MR. HODGE & MR. HAZARD

Mr. Hodge & Mr. Hazard

ELINOR WYLIE

"Why, let the stricken deer go weep,
The hart ungallèd play;
For some must watch while some must sleep:
Thus runs the world away."

Academy Chicago Publishers

Published in 1984 by
Academy Chicago, Publishers
425 N. Michigan Ave.
Chicago, IL 60611

Library of Congress Cataloging in Publication Data

Wylie, Elinor, 1885-1928.
    Mr. Hodge & Mr. Hazard.

    Reprint. Originally published: New York: A. Knopf, 1928.

    I. Title.
PS3545.Y45M5   1984   813'.52   84-14560
ISBN 0-89733-113-3 (pbk.)

FOR
Helen

THE author of the following little romance begs that the reader will accept it as a work of fiction pure and simple, nor seek to discover within its pages portraits of dead or living persons. The central character may indeed be regarded as a composite miniature of the whole generation of early nineteenth century romantics, but reduced to so small a scale and depicted in colours so subdued as to render the like-nesses invisible. No attempt has been made either to conceal or to emphasize the traits of the unlucky type to which Mr.

Advertisement

Hazard belongs and whose imperfections he may serve to illustrate. He was evidently the victim of an excessive sensibility which the high order of his talents failed to stiffen into character. With gifts and natural abilities far above the common, he nevertheless lacked the power of self-discipline to a regrettable degree, and therefore fell an easy prey to morbid introspection and the disapproval of Mr. Hodge.

The author would be sorry to burden the illustrious shoulders of any genius with the hollow pack of Mr. Hazard's opinions; his eccentricities are his own, and if she has purloined a pistol ball or a black felt hat from his contemporary or hers she hopes to be forgiven. She has formed this little image of an idealist from various clays, and if, like the sculptor of a figurine, she has used an armature to uphold the practicable stuff, she believes the expedient justified. The novel of Mr. Hodge and Mr. Hazard is an everyday fable; its historical trappings are slight, and it must remain not a disguised biography but a brief symbolic romance of the mind.

Contents

Book One

MR. HAZARD

Book Two

THE YOUNG HUNTINGS

Contents

Book Three

MR. HODGE

Contents

Book One

MR. HAZARD

MR. HAZARD

I

Funeral of a Mouse

WHEN MR. HAZARD was forty years old, he
decided to revisit England. Having been
out of it for precisely fifteen years, he had half forgotten its climate; his memory was incurably romantic, and through veils of far-away mist he saw
the blackthorn more clearly than the mud. Also,
it was true that he, who so dearly loved the sun,

had been rather too much in the sun of late. Greece had been fever and chills by turns, and the cave of the chief Odysseus a very rack for broken bones. Missolonghi had been hot in the month of April 1824; a distinguished poet had perished there, and another, less distinguished, had merely had malaria and miraculously neglected to die of it. The month of May 1825 had been execrably hot, even in the grotto upon the slopes of Mount Parnassus, in the captious opinion of a man mortally wounded. The temperature of such a man has a tropical noon of its own.

If, like Mr. Hazard, you are mortally wounded and yet remain alive, you haven't been mortally wounded after all; you have only the doubtful satisfaction of knowing that there is a pistol ball somewhere behind your collar-bone. In the wet February of 1833 Mr. Hazard began to derive a perverse but gentle pleasure from the conviction that if he continued to grow thinner, he might soon be able to see the pistol ball as plainly as the collar-bone while he shaved by candlelight. He had never yet learned to button his night-shirt properly at the neck.

He had half forgotten the English climate when he landed at London Docks; the channel fogs had been clean as new milk compared to this tarnished verdigris smoke from which the face of his friend Hartleigh emerged with looming eyes like the spread wings of a soft dilapidated bat. The little man was shabby; his coat shared a certain worn furry look with his hair and thick eyelashes.

"My dear friend!" said Mr. Hazard; ten years ago, in Italy, he had cried "My dearest friend!" but now he lacked the requisite breath for the superlative syllable. The fog was heavy as sea-water in his lungs, and a hundred times dirtier in its taste and smell.

"My dear fellow; my dear Hazard!" said Mr. Hartleigh; the beads of fog upon his thick shabby eyelashes grew more salty as he spoke. "And quite, quite unchanged since last we met; what happiness to see you still unchanged!"

"Hah!" said Mr. Hazard incredulously; it was his new way of laughing, which Mr. Hartleigh had never heard before. He supposed, accurately enough, that Hazard had picked it up in

Greece; he concluded that modern Greek must be a harsh inhuman tongue.

"That was in '23, before we sailed for the Ionian Islands, I believe," said Mr. Hazard; "I should have thought, you know, that you'd notice a slight difference . . . however, you are yourself looking remarkably well." Which was so palpably untrue that he hastened to add: "And how is the excellent Annamaria?"

"Her health is good at the present moment; considering, you understand," said Mr. Hartleigh to Mr. Hazard, who perfectly understood. He had known Annamaria for a great many years.

"Those delightful winters in Spain and Arabia, with your wife and dear little Lionel," said Mr. Hartleigh, who was oppressed by the silence and by Mr. Hazard's large black hat, "how you must have enjoyed them! Of what inestimable benefit must they have been to your health! And Egypt, too; what did you think of the pyramids? I had hoped you would let me have a sonnet to the pyramids for the *Gossip*."

"Do you mind if I let down the window a bit?" asked Mr. Hazard. They were now in the hackney-coach; it was undoubtedly an extravagance, but since it was wordlessly agreed between them that the extravagance was Mr. Hazard's, nobody cared in the least about the money. Mr. Hazard was beginning to care rather painfully about the smell; the fancy visited him that the corpse of a mouse might be travelling to London with them in this extravagant hackney-coach.

Mr. Hartleigh glanced fearfully at Mr. Hazard, surprised again by the new and inhuman accent in his voice. "An unmelodious tongue, the modern Greek," thought Mr. Hartleigh in iambic pentameter. Having glanced once more at Mr. Hazard, he decided, not unreasonably, that his friend was about to faint. At the moment they were passing within the curdled nimbus of a street-lamp; Mr. Hartleigh perceived with warm-hearted concern that Mr. Hazard was precisely the colour of a vellum lectionary of the fifteenth century. A few ghostly freckles still lingered upon the thin bridge of his nose, but even these had changed from russet into dun. It was a truly shocking revelation; Mr. Hartleigh let down the window with a bang.

Mr. Hazard said: "Thank you; I prefer the fog to the mouse, don't you?" Mr. Hartleigh realized that Mr. Hazard had not the least intention of fainting; his words were clear and dry as scraps of mica.

Mr. Hartleigh, who had taken a small silver-plated flask from his pocket, put it back again with a thrifty sigh of relief.

"I thought you were ill, but happily it was but the unnatural hue of the fog," he said, his kindly eyes looming bat-like through the dusk.

"It is but the natural hue of my face, unhappily," said Mr. Hazard without apparent regret. "This is the celebrated Missolonghi tint, half-way between tallow and ship's biscuit. A really hot Arabian sun may toast the biscuit to a more agreeable brown, but this confounded voyage has turned it into toast-and-water. I assure you that I am quite well; I am only concerned lest Annamaria be annoyed with me for sacrificing my appearance to my principles."

"She is certain to admire you; you have the air of a distinguished foreigner," said Mr. Hartleigh, laughing. He was glad that his friend

Hazard was not after all about to faint in a hackney-coach, and sincerely glad he had not wasted his brandy upon a fellow who did not care whether he drank cognac or cowslip wine.

Mr. Hazard said: "Hah!" which to Mr. Hartleigh's imagination had become modern Greek for a proper English chuckle; he pulled his large black hat over his large and rather alarming eyes and promptly fell asleep. Within the hackney-coach Mr. Hartleigh alone preserved his sharp and waking faculties; the corpse of the mouse and the slumbering form of Mr. Hazard travelled up to London in a darkling stillness equal and profound.

2

A Coffin in the Neighbourhood

AMONG MR. HAZARD'S several sorts of genius, sombre and luminous by turns, the power of making himself uncomfortable lay shining and singular. Undoubtedly the gift of the most malicious of all his fairy godmothers, it remained a wicked talisman which invariably conducted him to the hardest arm-chair, the smokiest reading-lamp,

and the coldest cup of tea. It was his lifelong
habit to pour the tea out while it was still too
weak, and this from natural impatience; an equally
natural absence of mind prevented him from drinking it until he had read another chapter or written
another stanza. Thus he never drank any but
tepid tea, and the large ungenial cup which he
lifted to his lips that evening at eleven o'clock was
perhaps the chilliest in England.

It was as much Mr. Hartleigh's fault as Mr.
Hazard's. Annamaria had given it to them boiling
hot and almost black, but while the one gulped,
choked, and proceeded with his pathetic narra-
tive, the other sat, unmoving and apparently unmoved, until his friend had explained the failure
of the *Gossip* down to its last distressing detail.
Then he sipped his cold poison reflectively and
spoke.

"But what did you expect, Hartleigh?" he
asked in his new inhuman voice, which was chilly
and bitter as the tea.

Mr. Hartleigh had expected anything but
this cruel question; he had expected sympathy
at the very least for the old venture, and possibly

something more substantial for future trials of his perseverance as an editor.

"The difficulty of conducting a review . . ." began Mr. Hartleigh, and talked steadily for an hour by the stained ormolu clock. At the end of this period it struck seven and roused Annamaria from her nap. She sat up on the worn red velvet couch; one of Annamaria's cheeks was redder than the couch and impressed with the stamped pattern of its velvet.

"That means it's midnight," she said, with a polite yawn.

Mr. Hazard opened his eyes very wide and stared at the clock; the solitary hand pointed to twelve.

"So it's quite impossible to tell the hour, ever, I suppose," he murmured sadly.

"Not a bit of it," said Annamaria, "I know its tricks by heart. The children will be home any minute; they've gone to a little party. Quite simple; a country cousin at the pianoforte and custards for supper, but they enjoy it. They are cheerful young people; you'll make friends with them again in no time."

"I hope so," said Mr. Hazard. "They are too grown-up now to want me to pretend that I'm a savage creature; I needn't pretend that now, need I?"

"Of course not, Hazard; they're too old."

"I'm too old, Annamaria; it has become a work of supererogation," said Mr. Hazard.

"What does he mean, Hartleigh?" Annamaria inquired a trifle pettishly; she was dazed by sleep and possibly by something else.

"He means that he's already a savage creature, which is manifestly absurd; he is the tenderest-hearted man alive," said Hartleigh, loyal to the past, and hopeful for the future of the new review.

"What makes you think I am alive?" asked Mr. Hazard alarmingly, twisting the locks above his brow into the same unicorn's horn which used to delight and frighten the Hartleigh children out of their wits sixteen years before. Only it was not quite the same unicorn's horn, after all, for now it was the colour of silver instead of the colour of bronze.

"Have you found a coffin for me in the neighbourhood?" asked Mr. Hazard. "You promised me faithfully in your last letter that you'd find a bed for me in the neighbourhood. Savage creatures hate being bothers to their friends, if they're lucky enough to have any." He rose from the hardest of the arm-chairs and stood looking at Hartleigh and Annamaria; you could see from the expression in his eyes that he thought he was smiling.

"My dear fellow!" cried Hartleigh in genuine distress; his thick furry eyelashes blinked back a tear.

"Hazard, I wish you would not talk so wildly; you terrify me," said Annamaria rather unjustly, since Mr. Hazard had spoken with the most frigid calm. "I think you must be ill; certainly you look shockingly ill. You are not yourself; it is quite unlike you to terrify a woman."

"My dear Annamaria, you do not know me in my present incarnation; I terrify every woman who beholds me, or even hears my voice. You remember me as a herd-neglected deer; now I am a wolf or a mad dog. An interesting example of metempsychosis. But I am very sorry to have frightened you; please forgive me."

"Ah, Hazard, it is nothing; I was only afraid

= 13 =

that you were ill," cried Annamaria warmly; her kindness, like the red velvet couch, was worn but serviceable. "Sit down again and let me give you a glass of port and a nice Bath Oliver before you go; I remember well how fond you used to be of Bath Olivers. Yes, we have found you quite a comfortable room, and only two streets away from us. You must have a good sleep, and in the morning you will have forgotten all that nonsense about wolves."

"Yes, yes," insisted Mr. Hartleigh. "In the morning you must breakfast here; you will see all the children, and we shall be a very cheerful little gathering. You need a good night's sleep to cure you of these melancholy and erroneous ideas about yourself. In the morning you will be completely rested."

"How pleasant it would be," said Mr. Hazard, with averted eyes, which pretended to look at the clock while they really looked at the fire, "if what you so kindly say could come true; if in the morning I should have forgotten all this nonsense about wolves, and should find myself completely rested."

3

Warm Wine and Water

"You should have gone with him, Hartleigh," said Annamaria five minutes later. "He obviously isn't fit to go about alone. I think we shall both of us be struck dumb for the lies we told him; I was between laughing and crying when you swore to heaven that he was handsomer than ever. He never was, to my way of thinking, but now! Lord, I never saw such a dreadful alteration in my life! Why, the man looks half dead and wholly mad; you should have gone with him to his lodgings, if only for poor Mrs. Downing's sake. She will think him the devil, ringing her bell at midnight in that extraordinary hat."

Mr. Hartleigh poured out a second glass of port, the one which Mr. Hazard had not taken; Annamaria had the other decanter to herself, and that decanter's contents might easily have been sherry.

"I should have offended him, my love," he said meekly. "It was quite evident that he wished to go alone; he knows this part of Marylebone well, and I am not seriously alarmed for Mrs. Downing's peace of mind. I by no means agree with you about Hazard's ill-looks; he has endured great hardships in the past, as you know, and doubtless the fatigues of the journey and the agitations of his return to his native land have told upon him. But he has lost none of his elegance and distinction; he is thinner, of course, but the carving of the brow and cheek-bones is finer than ever; it is a beautiful head."

"Beautiful!" cried Annamaria rather shrilly; she was tired and cross, and beginning to be worried about the children. "If he is beautiful, then I am the Venus Anadyomene!"

"Not necessarily, Annamaria; the fancy is pleasing, but unfortunately it does not follow. It is a pity; it would be delightful if the thing were not *non sequitur*, for I assure you that Hazard is beautiful," said her husband, who in spite of his small vulgarities was a person of taste.

"Don't forget that I tried to model him in clay; he has not a regular feature," said Annamaria. "Put a few more coals upon the fire, will you? I think I hear the children coming; they will be wanting hot wine and water, I suppose, but we ought not to afford it."

"As well attempt to model Mercury in batter pudding, my dear; you might try quicksilver next time. Ah, forgive me if I've hurt your feelings; it's a great temptation to catch a flying likeness of him. His wife has tried it in her novels, over and over again."

"And failed," said Annamaria. "I don't want to be spiteful, but she does nag him, you know. You've said yourself that she'll never understand him; that she's too much like Baddeley to appreciate him."

"She's Baddeley's own daughter, to be sure; we must remember not to abuse the old villain now that Hazard's come home. He's so absurdly generous that he may still admire Baddeley." Mr. Hartleigh put the bits of coal upon the fire one by one, delicately, as if they had been lumps of sugar dropped into a fragile teacup.

"It wasn't the children after all; it must have been those rowdy young people next door," said Annamaria as disapprovingly as if her own children had never made a noise. "Hazard's come home; ah well, one can hardly call it that, poor fellow, can one?"

"I suppose not; Mrs. Downing's rooms are clean but cheerless, and he will never in this sad world demand a fire at midnight. The fog's worse than ever; I wish we need not have sent him forth from our cozy hearthside," murmured Mr. Hartleigh, relinquishing the poker and coaxing the frugal blaze with a folded newspaper.

The flames brightened under his fostering care; the lamp, turned thriftily low, diffused a softer light over the warm untidy room. Unlike Mrs. Downing's lodgings, the place was neither clean nor cheerless; it preserved a certain air of muddled comfort in the midst of shabbiness and confusion. The books had climbed up the walls to the very top to escape the litter of undarned stockings upon the couch, the pile of inky proof upon the table, the leaves of foolscap paper scattered underfoot. The stockings were white and gray and black, the couch was faded red, the arm-chairs were mustard colour, the curtains and the lamp-shade were a lively crimson, the table-cover combined these tints in a tapestry pattern.

Mr. Hartleigh, who had presented it to Anna-maria as a birthday gift, thought it rather like the table-cover in "The Eve of Saint Agnes." "A cloth of woven crimson, gold and jet"; yes, that was an exquisite description of the tapestry pattern, in Mr. Hartleigh's opinion.

"Cozy; very cozy; I wish with all my soul that he need not have fled away into the storm," sighed Mr. Hartleigh, with his mind still upon "The Eve of Saint Agnes."

"Storm, Hartleigh? There isn't a sign of a storm, though the fog's thicker than ever," said Annamaria, peering between the curtains. "It's too bad of those boys not to take better care of their sisters; I told them half past twelve at latest. Sometimes I think them quite irresponsible, I do indeed." She spoke as indignantly as if she had not been used all her life to irresponsible people.

"You see, my dear," she went on, taking up an irresponsible boy's sock and throwing it down again when she saw that both heel and toe were completely destroyed, "I didn't mean this sort of home for Hazard when I said you couldn't call it home for the poor fellow. If he leaves his wife and child in a castle in Spain, he can't expect this sort of home. I meant that with his family refusing to recognize him, and with Baddeley in a black fury, and his friends Piggott and Bird each absorbed in a mistress or a wife, England may be very cold comfort for him. And we can do so little, in these circumstances; it isn't like Hampstead, when he was a young and promising poet. If only your book on Lord Alonzo had been a success!"

"Annamaria, I asked you never to mention that detestable subject again; I hope I am as reasonable about reviews as most men, but the ferocity of those attacks . . . pray don't remind me of them. As to Hazard, of course all those Cambridge fellows admire and respect him deeply; you may depend upon it that they will seek him out at the earliest opportunity."

"If he depends upon it, he will be disappointed, my love. What is the Cambridge Union, to begin with?" asked Annamaria sharply.

"Shall I explain it to you?" Mr. Hartleigh inquired with a harmless trace of irony.

"Certainly not; you know very well what I

mean. What good can that ridiculous perform-
ance do him now? And then, he was beaten by
seventy votes; a disgrace, I call it, to be publicly
declared a lesser poet than that wretch Alonzo
Raven. It is worse even than what happened to
Shelley."

"*De mortuis*, Annamaria . . . please do not
remind me of a painful subject. Poor Hazard!
We must see what we can do for him. Perhaps
Hallam . . ."

"It's quite hopeless, Hartleigh. A few years
have probably turned several hot-headed Cambridge undergraduates into respectable fathers of
families. There is a great prejudice against him
still; what would happen if they introduced him
to their wives?"

"The usual thing, my dear; their wives would
fall in love with him," answered Mr. Hartleigh
with a smile.

His wife was peering between the crimson
curtains. She lifted the window a little, and a
thin wave of fog slid into the room like a yellow
wraith.

"There are the children at last," she cried,

"They are just turning the corner. How very disobedient they are, to be sure! I suppose, since it is so late, I shall be teased into letting them have their wine and water."

4

Ambush at a Breakfast-table

MR. HAZARD's genius for making himself uncomfortable did not stop short of terrestrial immensities; its tempests were not confined to teacups, and its unkind enchantments were capable of plucking the waves up to heaven by their streaming hair and dissolving the skies, reversed within the Bay of Biscay. Earthquakes padded by his side like faithful heavy-footed beasts, and white unmoving glaciers shivered in his presence like tides beneath the moon. One of the lighter thunderstrokes of this tormenting magic was laid upon him when he chose to revisit London during an epidemic of influenza.

The fact that he had failed to go to Paris during the cholera epidemic of the previous year can only be explained by his deep-rooted dislike of France and the bitter disillusionment he had suffered over the Revolution of 1830. Among the nomadic tribes of Arabia he had been regarded with veneration because of his apparent power of attracting and subduing sand-storms, and now that he had left his wife and little Lionel safe in San Sebastian, he felt confident that there would be fair weather and softly blowing winds along the Spanish coast during such time as he should spend in England. Many captains of East India-men had good cause to be grateful to Mr. Hazard during these months of lingering winter and of early island spring.

When he breakfasted with the Hartleighs upon the following morning, the influenza had already set its stigmata upon him. Annamaria marked the vivid flush upon his cheek-bones and the abnormal brilliance of his eyes and trembled for her children's health. There was small use in worrying over Hazard's health, because obviously he hadn't any, but the children were different; they were young and strong and their cheeks were suffused by a wholesome permanent pink and not by the uncertain colour of a flame. At the same moment she reflected that Hazard's eyes were unorthodox and rather appalling. Annamaria felt she could not call them fine; fine eyes were shaded velvet, like dear Hartleigh's. Hazard's eyes disconcerted her; they were too bright for a domestic breakfast-table. Annamaria knew that if she were to take the pretty Sheffield salt-cellar and fling its contents upon the fire, the variable flames would be tortured for a fleeting instant into the colour of Hazard's eyes.

The girls were chattering happily of the galop, and of the meringues which had so fortunately replaced the expected custards at the party. "And claret-cup," said the girls, "lovely, with bits of pineapple in it!" The boys were occupied with their bacon and eggs; they would none of them eat porridge any longer, now that they were grown up.

"I must give them a dose of quinine all around," thought Annamaria, and wondered if the younger ones would still expect currant jelly afterwards.

Hartleigh was eating a small kipper; the little man blinked his soft furry eyelashes and peered at Hazard, thinking that the poor fellow looked wonderfully recovered. "He appears quite his old self this morning," thought Hartleigh with innocent satisfaction, dissecting his kipper.

Mr. Hazard noticed nothing whatever; he drank his tea and did not like it, and forgot to eat the food with which Annamaria provided him. He thought that the night had been unseasonably hot for the time of year, and was vaguely aware that he felt rather as if he had been climbing a very steep mountain. He should, by sad experience, have learned a fever to match every dead and living language that he knew, but he could not remember them so well as he remembered the languages, and he had never expected the influenza to meet him in England. The influenza was an Italian fever.

"Were you cold last night, Hazard?" Annamaria asked him accusingly.

Mr. Hazard started violently, and dropped the copy of *Corn-Law Rhymes* which he had just opened. "Yes," he said, "I found it extremely cold at first, before the weather changed; do you often have these extraordinary changes nowadays?"

"I knew it," cried Annamaria, between triumph and disgust. "Hazard, you have the influenza; you'll have to go home and go to bed at once."

"Nothing of the sort," protested Hartleigh. "He's looking remarkably well, and, moreover, I wish to discuss the Reform Bill with him. Pray don't interfere with us, my love; it is most important that we discuss the Reform Bill without further loss of time. Also, he's already promised to write a pamphlet advising the Government . . ."

"Stuff and nonsense," said Annamaria, "I tell you he has the influenza. I wish we could find a bed for you here, Hazard, but there are the children to be considered. They mustn't catch it from you, you know, and unluckily it's highly infectious."

Mr. Hazard heard her words quite plainly, but at first they conveyed nothing to his truly remarkable intelligence save an impression that he was again in Greece and that someone had shot at him with an old-fashioned fowling-piece from behind a silver-plated tea-urn. But in Greece the ambush had been a clump of flowering laurel, and the report had been deadened by the long melody of waves breaking along a beach curved like an ivory crescent. The clump of flowering laurel had been far away, and only a stinging score of pellets had lodged in his shoulder and in the thin arm thrown so instinctively over the clear discerning eyes, which had seen the smoke like a tree of white blossoms rising above the rosy laurel. Now it was too late to cover his eyes against the ambushed shot. Stupid of him, not to have seen the white prophetic cloud above the tea-urn!

"You've startled him, Annamaria," said Mr. Hartleigh, "and he can't possibly have the influenza in Mrs. Downing's lodging-house."

"Of course I can," said Mr. Hazard, rising swiftly from the breakfast-table. The extreme quickness of his wits had unwound the delirious tangle of his nerves; his soul felt cold and sharp as an icicle within the skin and bone of his body, and behind his hot forehead his brain was frosty crystal.

"I'm sorry, Hazard," said Annamaria plaintively; the tears in her eyes made Mr. Hazard's unsubstantial figure waver and grow translucent like a ghost, "I hate to let you go; it's only for the children's sake. Hartleigh shall walk to Mrs. Downing's with you, and I'll send my doctor to you at once; one of the boys can take a message. I know you don't want any harm to come to the children because of you . . ."

"Good God!" said Mr. Hazard softly, and walked from the room in the implicit belief that he had taken leave of everyone according to the most rigid forms of etiquette in use among the Grecian chieftains.

"Don't come with me, Hartleigh; I beg of you not to come with me now," he said to Mr. Hartleigh in the narrow brown tunnel of the passage. "I assure you I shall be quite safe. They have most of them gone to Salona, and there is an enchanting moon tonight like the zone of a young virgin."

He gazed at Mr. Hartleigh coolly and haughtily; his eyes were clear as sea-water under his burning brows. If he did not speak precisely as the frosty crystal of his brain directed, it was because of the brightness of the crescent moon in his eyes. The innermost essence of his being, congealed into ice, longed coldly to be quit of Mr. Hartleigh.

5

Dried Peas and Rusty Needles

LONG, long before Mr. Hazard was an atheist, or a Platonist, or a pantheist, he was declared regenerate, and grafted into the body of Christ's Church. The airy fine-spun feathers of an infant's hair were warily and discreetly wetted for the mystical washing away of sin; the infant's forehead, fragile as the shell wherefrom an eagle may be born, was duly signed with the cross of Christ's flock. Of the efficacy of this christening his impulsive youth could never be persuaded; the subtle convolutions of his later mind must ever be illumined by an intellectual beam peculiar to himself. In the opinion of the many that prayer had remained unanswered which desired for him power and strength to have victory, and to triumph, against the devil, the world, and the flesh. All things belonging to the spirit might live and grow in him, but they must grow alone, without the approval of the elect, or the help of his godfathers and godmothers in baptism.

Therefore it is improbable that Mr. Hazard had studied the second chapter of the Gospel according to Saint Matthew with special diligence for the past thirty-five years; it is a brilliant instance of his high powers of memory that all at once he seemed to have the thing by heart. He had been cruelly shaken by the brief struggle of wills between himself and the little man who had insisted upon taking his arm in the street; outwardly he had been glacially composed, but once or twice he had felt the icicle of his inmost soul shiver and crack with the sick violence of despair. Nevertheless he had won; the little man had turned and left him abruptly, with something like a blessing uttered in the voice which most people reserve for oaths. Mr. Hazard had watched him out of sight, coldly marvelling at the broken droop of his shoulders and at the dinginess of the handkerchief with which he seemed to be mopping his soft shabby eyes.

Mr. Hazard knew that his own eyes were hard; the strength of his will had kept them hard as flint or the blue fabric of the pole itself while they stared scornfully at the little man who was talking of friendship and quinine and mustard foot-baths. But now they were no longer flint; they were red-hot steel in the hollows of his skull.

Mr. Hazard rejoiced to know that he had remained composed and haughty during his spiritual battle with the little man, but he also knew what secret agonies and agitations had strained his nerves and plucked his heart-strings to a hideous discord. He looked at the house; the steps appeared giddily steep, and at the end of their unnatural perspective the door was an ambiguous colour. He decided that he had far better walk to Hampstead.

Suddenly he remembered everything with precise and delicate clarity; he remembered the breakfast-table at the Hartleighs, and the silver-plated tea-urn, stained rosy as an apple on the side where the firelight touched it, and the breakfast china, which was half willow-pattern crockery and half pink lustre ware, and the kippers and the bacon, and the greengage jam which the girls had wished were apricot. He remembered

Annamaria's purple stuff gown, and Hartleigh's worn brown jacket, and their two faces, one so red and one so pasty. And he remembered the grownup children's smiling faces, florid or sallow as their parents' types inclined them, and the solemn faces of the younger children who had not yet been given their cups of tea. He remembered the musty astringent taste of his own cup of tea, and he even remembered the poached egg shrunk thin upon his plate, wrinkled like a winter puddle. He had not seen it at the time, but now he remembered its horrid chilliness, and his burning mind shuddered at the memory. The whole was a *genre* picture, varnished brightly by the fever in his blood.

He remembered that he had the influenza, and that some of the plump and smiling children might even now nourish the seeds of it within their solid flesh. Annamaria had known quite well that he was the enemy of children; that he cast a blight upon them, that they withered in his presence like murdered flowers.

The Hartleigh children were not like flowers, yet Annamaria was right; it was not fair that they should die. And what of those other children who had died; were they not each one like a flower or a bird, and was it not his fault that they were dead? Or was it, perhaps, the fault of the Lord Chancellor?

The most exquisite images, the pure immortal music that the slight stops of human breath evolve from language, the extremest dizzying flight of thought into the void, were all imprisoned and confused within the agony of Mr. Hazard's mind. The exaltation, the mercurial elegance, the valour, and the strong vivacity were shrivelled up by fever until they rattled in his head like scorching peas and fled along his veins like rusty needles. He was in pain, but whether of the body or the soul his fever could not tell.

"Then Herod, when he saw that he was mocked of the wise men, was exceeding wroth, and sent forth, and slew all the children that were in Bethlehem, and in all the coasts thereof . . ." The harsh and breaking voice was Mr. Hazard's.

Mr. Hazard knew that he was not really Herod; he had been Herod for a little while in the thick fog, and he had pitied the king because the crown was heavy and brutal as it weighed upon his brow. They had tried to make Mr. Hazard King of Greece after Alonzo Raven had perished miserably of fever at Missolonghi. Now Mr. Hazard himself was perishing miserably of fever in Poland Street, Oxford Road. He was not in Hampstead after all; he was in Poland Street, standing before the house where he had lodged when he was first expelled from the university. He remembered the pattern of trellises and green vine-leaves upon the walls, and how the fancy that the rooms were summer arbours had delighted his solitude.

He felt intelligent and sane and desperately tired. He refused to admit even to his own mind that he felt ill, but there can be no reasonable doubt that he felt very ill indeed. The fact that he walked slowly to Oxford Road and crawled into a cab must be conclusive proof of this, even without the additional evidence of his visit to a chemist's shop, where he purchased a small bottle of quinine pilules and rejected a quantity of excellent advice. His restored senses accomplished the journey to Mrs. Downing's front door, whose ambiguous colour had faded to a dirty buff.

Mrs. Downing met him upon the doorstep; the cabman was relieved, but Mr. Hazard was wearily fretted by her presence. He essayed to pass her with three syllables of apology.

"Mr. Hartleigh and the doctor's been and gone this half hour," she informed him sternly. "I think, sir, that the doctor was a bit put out. He says as you're to go to bed immejitly, and he's coming back at ten o'clock tomorrow morning."

"Thank you," said Mr. Hazard. He leaned against the iron railing of the steps and wished that she would let him pass.

"Will you be wanting any supper?" asked Mrs. Downing indignantly. "They said something about broth, but you'd have to have a soup-bone in for that, sir."

"No, thank you," said Mr. Hazard faintly, and fled to his room.

Here was no arbour of vine-leaves, but a travesty of roses traced in soot upon the walls. The counterpane's unclean design was like a nest of serpents. Mr. Hazard decided not to go to bed.

He sat upon the most uncomfortable chair, reading Mr. Tennyson's *Poems, Chiefly Lyrical* without any perceptible sensation of pleasure. His head ached abominably, and although he sat in his greatcoat, he was very cold.

Presently he could read no longer. While the chill shook his bones asunder, like breakable dice in a black dice-box, he lay staring out of the window into the impenetrable emptiness of the fog, wishing that the exaltation and valour of his mind had not been shrivelled up into scorched peas and rusty needles.

When at last he had survived the night and its delirium, he knew that the influenza could never kill him.

6

Specific for a Fever

"What have you done with your hat, sir?" asked Mrs. Downing the next Sunday afternoon, as Mr. Hazard ascended her steps. It was all too true; his head was uncovered in the mild February twilight, which might so easily have been April had the trees been green instead of smoky lavender in the dusk. The church-bells were ringing in a circle around them, as cuckoos cry from every point of the compass, but with a solemn harmony of echo in their sound. It did not seem fitting to Mrs. Downing that Mr. Hazard should walk in the street with uncovered head while all the neighbouring church-bells rang to evensong. At the same time she hoped that his other hat, if he had one, would be smaller and paler than the satanic thing he had always worn pulled down over his eyes, as if he feared his eyes would frighten children.

"There is another hat exactly like it in the little corded box," said Mr. Hazard nonchalantly; he had not the faintest idea what he had done with the original hat. He believed that he might possibly have given it in lieu of sixpence to the cross-eyed fiddler who had been playing such melancholy music under a bow-window in Half-Moon Street. Certainly the fellow had held a black felt hat in his hand as Mr. Hazard strode away towards Piccadilly.

"The Half-Moon revisited," said Mr. Hazard to his own soul. "A fine Sunday afternoon spent among the sarcophagi of my dead selves. But at least I shall have missed the doctor." He spoke the last sentence aloud, and cheerfully.

"Yes, he's been and gone again, sir, and in a towering rage. He says he's finished with you, sir, and that you're bound to die, but Mr. Hartleigh made him leave a tranquillizing draught in hopes it would make you change your mind." Mrs. Downing spoke kindly; she liked Mr. Hazard much better now that he had taken her first floor sitting-room to hold the books which had been packed in the three larger corded boxes.

Mr. Hazard had managed his influenza very cleverly after all. Finding that the doctor affected his nerves to a wire-drawn extremity which had much in common with severe neuralgia he had avoided him by brilliant guess-work, and a series of long walks. The strangling bow-string of a sore throat, the obstinate helmet of pain clipping his temples, were evils slight and transitory compared to the dull aching lethargy to which the doctor's voice subdued him like a blow. Thus, in prolonged escapes, he had plenty of fresh air, and for the rest he contrived to exist upon tea and quinine and the peculiar tough and cindery toast which was the specialty of Mrs. Downing's kitchen.

The fatigues of this life of flights and evasions were numerous and at times excessive. Mr. Hazard frequently found it difficult to collect the strength to get up after a bad night, but as he took infinite pains and employed a variety of ingenious shifts and dodges, he was generally far upon his way by nine o'clock of the rainiest morning. Sunlight might waken his vitality half an hour earlier, but his own invention never failed to pull the scattered pieces of his faculties together in time to elude his foe.

No one ever knew where he went; he revisited every house wherein he had lodged during his vanished years in London, but even Mr. Hazard could not walk for ever in the rain with fever in his bones, and it is probable that he must occasionally have slept in the pews of churches, in the parlours of inns, and among the musty recesses of obscure book-shops. Wherever he went, he never went to the Hartleighs.

Once, to his intense and cold annoyance, he

was brought home insensible in a costermonger's cart from Covent Garden Market, where he had wandered in an eccentric search for Roman hyacinths. Again, at stagnant midnight, he emerged from the emblazoned doors of a superb private carriage; he was pale and quivering with scorn, which, like a flame of the pit, consumed him to his hurt and wore him away to a proud skeleton. He thanked the owner of the carriage in words of exquisite politeness impregnate with vinegar and brimstone.

"I am afraid I have had the misfortune to offend him," said the owner of the carriage, a slim and merry gentleman with auburn curls. "He fainted under my horses' hoofs; evidently he had preferred death to my poor assistance, but, being unconscious, he could not tell me so, and I made the excusable error of saving him. Pray tender him my compliments and apologies, and assure him of my willingness to drive a coach and four over him at his earliest convenience." And he gave Mrs. Downing a card engraved with a great name and a little coronet.

If Mr. Hazard suffered, in these adventures

or in solitude, no one but himself was the wiser or the sorrier for that suffering. He avoided the Hartleighs as if they had been orpiment or aqua Tofana; the fear of infecting them with influenza had become an obsession with him, and he saw himself as poison to their domestic peace. Poor Hartleigh, who was sincerely attached to Mr. Hazard, visited Mrs. Downing's front door every day with touching futility; she was instructed never to admit him to the house. Now and then he had the good or evil luck to waylay Mr. Hazard in the street; he soon grew convinced of his friend's approaching dissolution and of the serious derangement of his exalted mind.

"Those incomparable powers," said Hartleigh to Annamaria, "quite, quite wasted. We must try to get him back to Spain and proper care. What a tragedy it is, to be sure!"

The incomparable powers of Mr. Hazard's mind were not really overthrown; in lucid and luminous intervals of evening light, in the divining crystal of the new morning, in the oracular silence of night, he perceived the universe and pierced it with the subtlest devices of the human soul. But not always; not at his worst moments, and hardly, even, at his middling moments.

This mild February afternoon, in which the church-bells cried like holy cuckoos from every point of the compass and from all the church towers between, was fair to middling, fair with an almost April fairness, and middling by the grace of a new moon. Nevertheless Mr. Hazard was very tired as he climbed the stair to his room; he wondered wearily why optimists like young Mr. Browning must hail unhappy poets by such titles as Sun-treader and the false and flattering like.

7

Camelopard at a Party

WHETHER Mr. Hazard had influenza three times or only once must remain a mystery insoluble by the arts of medicine, the cabbalistic Tarots, or transcendental magic. No one, and least of all Mr. Hazard himself, was ever competent to decide whether the plague descended upon his head in three separate storms, or, waxing and waning like the inconstant moon, companioned his mortal loneliness from February until May.

This loneliness, although extreme, was of the spirit rather than the flesh, and by this time Mr. Hazard had far more spirit than flesh wherewith to be lonely. His nerves were constantly excoriated by fear of meeting the Hartleigh children in the street, for he believed that he might breathe destruction upon them as if he were Jehovah and they the elder sons of the Egyptians, but otherwise he was careless of others and himself alike, and he permitted both Piggott and Bird to call upon him whenever they were in London, which was seldom enough. He refused to visit them in turn in the country, because there were children in their houses, and at his worst moments, with his head aching atrociously, he still remembered King Herod, whose crown was sharp and heavy about his brow.

Several Cambridge graduates made a point of showing him every possible attention; his pride made the nature of such attentions narrow and difficult as climbing pinnacles of ice, and most of these gentlemen soon wearied in well-meaning. Young Mr. Browning was different; he could not be fobbed off, and his devotion was both tigerish and mulish in its intensity. Neither the forked lightning flash of Mr. Hazard's scorn nor the frozen profundity of his indifference could keep Mr. Browning from building fires and boiling kettles; Mr. Hazard might occasionally have found him a comfort if his boots had ever lost their abominable *parvenu* habit of creaking.

Mrs. Norton discovered him almost at once, by some hazel wand of romantic intuition; she hoped that she had found the true Castalia among the stones of London. She was destined to be disappointed, but not before she had fallen in love with Mr. Hazard in a light Platonic way, fragile and sparkling as the Waterford wineglass brimming with champagne which she put into his thin hand. A few drops of champagne were spilled upon Mr. Hazard's black coat; he set down the glass and forgot to drink the wine, as he forgot to avail himself of the mirth and kindliness in Mrs. Norton's lovely eyes. Mr. Norton was from home; the little drawing-room in Storey's Gate was gay with flowers.

"It was charming of you to come to my party, Mr. Hazard," said Mrs. Norton. "People tell me that you are harder to catch than a camel-opard."

It was at the giddy peak of Mr. Hazard's March influenza; the full moon of its fever cast its illumination upon his countenance, and every-one who had ever seen Mr. Hazard before de-clared that he was quite amazingly unchanged by fifteen years, that the silver in his hair was vastly becoming, and that he looked very young for his age. The colours of his youth were laid like a shining mask upon the worn contours of Mr. Hazard's face; nobody could deny his good looks.

"I could never have credited his eyes until I saw them," said Mrs. Norton. "But what fools they are who have called him gentle; he is the fiercest creature I ever beheld; he frightens me out of my wits, and without my wits I'm nothing."

She had her compliment, but not from Mr. Hazard. He knew that he was frightening Mrs. Norton, and therefore he refused to speak. He walked softly about, striving to subdue the bril-liance of his eyes, striving to subdue the burning spirit within the slight fabric of his body, striv-ing very patiently to contrive some veil, some fleece of lamb or delicate freckled deerskin, which might hide his soul.

He was glad that Mrs. Norton had called him a camelopard; it was a pleasanter form of metempsychosis than his own fancy concerning wolves.

"Do you know, Mr. Hazard," Mrs. Norton asked him in another vain and gallant attempt to make him talk, "that it was your continual references to the Wandering Jew which first inspired me to write *The Undying One?* Does not the responsibility weigh heavily upon your scrupulous conscience?"

Mr. Hazard, convinced that he was smiling, told her that the burden was an honourable one. He refused to say more, unaware that Mrs. Norton had a thousand times rather have been frightened by his words than disappointed by his silences. He listened while she told him of her enthusiastic intention of writing a poem upon child labour; his sincere interest was tinctured by delirium, and in the wild radiance of his eyes the lady read the inspiration which his lips withheld.

Mrs. Norton wore white satin, with camellias

in her shadowy hair; she felt so truly the spiritual bride of Mr. Hazard that she was startled when he left her. They sat together against a sombre velvet curtain, under the downcast marble face of Clytie; the fiery scintillation of their looks, their vital and uneven beauty, the grace and the excellent violence of humanity, made them appear more valuable by contrast with the Greek perfection of the lifeless stone.

"Must you go?" asked Mrs. Norton, with more regret than she considered it strictly decorous to express. She had not the least suspicion that Mr. Hazard was feeling rather desperately ill; his fever clothed the emaciation of his body with a garment of light.

"I am sorry to hear that you have been unwell," said Mrs. Norton. "You will, of course, take care of all that your friends hold justly precious." Her lovely eyes declared her the most affectionate of his friends.

"I will, of course," said Mr. Hazard; his voice was hoarse because he had the influenza, and ironical because he believed that there was little left of him which the most partial of his friends could regard as precious. Mrs. Norton found his odd voice agreeable, because she was lightly and platonically in love with him.

"Farewell, my dear friend," said Mrs. Norton when he left her upon the stroke of midnight. She wished he would not go, and yet the hour was a proper enchantment to win away a spiritual bridegroom.

"Good-bye," said Mr. Hazard; twenty years ago he might have echoed her farewell as she desired. Now his exhaustion closed his lips upon the single word; he believed that he smiled, he knew that he touched her hand, and with that fainting effort he was gone.

Mrs. Norton gazed after him; she had a justified suspicion that she would never see him again. Her lovely eyes were full of laughter and a light and sparkling distillation of despair.

"What did he say?" asked everyone who had ever seen Mr. Hazard before or even heard of him; they crowded about Mrs. Norton, smiling with a voracious curiosity which she suddenly found abhorrent.

"Did he speak of her?" "Of his wife . . . ?"

"No, I meant his first wife." "Does he expect his father to forgive him?" "What did he say of Alonzo Raven? He knew him well." "And the wards in Chancery; did both of them die?" "And had he not several other children? Are any of them living?" "But one was Raven's child, to be sure, Caroline." "I think him fascinating, though shockingly rude, my love."

"No, he scarcely spoke to me," said Mrs. Norton truthfully. "Perhaps he was composing an ode to my eyelashes, which I shall receive by the first post tomorrow, but I have a horrid notion that he was thinking of nothing nearer than Caucasus or Himalay. We agreed that it was ten thousand pities that Walter Scott was dead, and twenty thousand more that Doctor Arnold had ever been born. That is all, I vow upon my honour, except that I wonder why no one has ever told me how like a camelopard the creature is, a lithe and savage camelopard of the Libyan waste. No, I assure you, my sweet Henrietta, he said not a syllable about the entail."

8

Skeleton in Armour

IN April, when he shaved by cloudy sunshine instead of candlelight, the vision of the pistol ball behind his collar-bone had become quite clear to Mr. Hazard. It needed far less effort upon the part of his imagination than the simple act of shaving required of his hand. His inventive mind, vivid in the midst of a pure silver pallor of dawn, played conjuring tricks with the pistol ball until it danced in air, flew skyward like a bird to pierce the risen day, or fell into his breast like a morning star.

The days began with showers, shot through and through with points of waking light. The colours were a rainbow's, but the shapes of cloud lacked the calm symmetry of a rainbow's arch; the wind and the wilder bursts of rain drove them hither and thither across the sky. Unquiet sparks of ecstasy, smaller than the sun's reflection in a drop of rain, lit the capricious twilight of Mr. Hazard's thoughts. The influenza had blown upon the mirror of his mind and misted it with a sorrowful fog: now the unquiet sparks of ecstasy moved over his mind and scoured it to brightness.

Years of the severest lessons of adversity had rendered Mr. Hazard's outward composure so nearly flawless that the sharp lancet of his self-contempt was blunted upon its surface. This superhuman armour was divided by no clumsy cracks and joinings; rather it resembled a coat of flexible mail, a cool marvel of contrived providence, a knitting up of nerves into invulnerable proof. Mr. Hazard's skill had woven it; he might have been proud of its difficult fabric. Yet he disliked the thing. It was a tough and stringent shield against the world, but after all it was only a makeshift. Even if his own skin had been but a beggarly tissue, he missed it sadly. He wished he might have patched and mended its tatters to last him into eternity.

Mr. Hazard cut himself inconsiderably upon his light and narrow jaw-bone; he hated the ravaged looks of the thin skull-face in the glass. The pliant coat of mail was cross-grained upon his limbs. The nights were never deep enough; they were like shallow straw pallets under his uneasy slumbers. There was no velvet profundity of oblivion to soothe him to repose. He reflected that ever since he had been flayed alive, he had remained a wretched sleeper.

Today he was to dine with the Hartleighs; his influenza had departed upon the wings of the last snow-storm, taking with it King Herod's crown and half a stone of Mr. Hazard's body. The influenza had been unable to pick his bones to more purpose, since other fevers, called by the names of living tongues and the dead tongues of antiquity, had already tried their teeth upon him in the past. As it was, Mr. Hazard could ill spare those seven pounds of flesh.

People had been very kind, he supposed; to a herd-neglected deer even perfunctory attentions might have appeared a solace. But to a wolf or a mad dog such trifles were no more than a whistling of stones and a clattering of rusty tins at hunted heels. And now everyone was telling him that he must go back to Spain.

Mr. Hazard was not ready to go back to Spain; he could have tumbled his brown and gilded books, his black jackets, and his white shirts into the three boxes and corded them before another's slower pulses should have counted a hundred, but nevertheless he was not ready to go. He had been in England for nearly three months, and as yet he had done nothing. His plan when he landed at London Docks had been as plain as the map of a pirate's island drawn upon white vellum in the best India ink; now it was stained and ragged as though the cruel mutations of his fever had beaten upon it in cold rain and tropic heat. Yet he knew that he could still piece it together and decipher its characters if he tried.

He had followed a few of its arrows, drawn upon his memory in red or black, along those streets and squares where he had lodged in his youth. He had even, driven by a febrile impulse, walked swiftly across the bridge which spanned the little river in the park, and fled northward until exhaustion winged him neatly on Hampstead Heath and laid him asleep under an elm-tree. He had stood upon a terrace above the Thames, and watched its lights, like pearls dissolved in wine-coloured dusk, and wondered if it still flowed softly by the town of Gravelow and under the tall shadow of certain woods. And pursuing its course to the end of Cheyne Walk, he had beheld the great stream shrunk up into a straitened channel of green and silver, and the trees of Battersea lifted against the new moon into towers and battlements of April leaves. As the scene resumed its true proportions, he longed for the upper reaches of the river, which lay shallow as white ribbons among the grass.

Mr. Hazard regarded his thin face in the glass with an unjust dislike; his hair was thick, although its bronze was overlaid with silver; and his eyes were large and bright, although their sockets set their colour in the shade, as a cloud may darken the sea. For the rest, he might have sat for a romantic portrait of Yorick's skull, save that his nose was salient and pointed and his mouth too passionate and mobile for a mouth that has been stopped with dust.

He tied his black cravat with extreme care, and was glad that the fine linen of his shirt was starched so clearly and so delicately above the violent hammering of his heart. He believed that by these small vanities and disguises he might delude Annamaria into thinking him completely recovered; the fear of Annamaria's pity fretted his nerves as damp may fret the strings of a violin.

He brushed his satanic hat and stared defiantly at his own image in the mirror; he was silently challenging his face to betray him. His makeshift armour covered him adequately, but the mask upon his face was worn away to a brittle layer of pride. He did not trust it, in a glare of light, or under the bold scrutiny of Annamaria's pity.

Had Alonzo Raven been there in the flesh, he would undoubtedly have given his white eye-teeth to look precisely as his unfortunate friend Mr. Hazard looked at that moment. Mr. Hazard did not suspect this curious fantasy; had he been convinced of its truth he would not have cared a single steel button of the narrow waistcoat which was so obviously too wide for him. Nevertheless he looked a very elegant and lively ghost indeed as he turned from the ghostly image of himself in the mirror with a last defiant smile.

9

Sepulchral Moth

MR. HAZARD's liveliness had fled away in spectral laughter long before he had cracked a single walnut for the children or refused a single glass of Mr. Hartleigh's port. Annamaria might have forgiven him for not drinking his soup, for then he was talking rather wittily about "Yarrow Revisited," but it was impossible to forgive him for not eating his dessert, for then he was silent and listless while Hartleigh chattered about reform. Mr. Hazard seemed to have lost his appetite for politics together with his appetite for almonds and raisins. His elegance remained to him, but it was a graveyard elegance little to Annamaria's florid taste. "A moth of which a coffin might have been the chrysalis"; someone had written that from Venice in a letter to Mr. Peacock. Perhaps the writer had been thinking of gondolas, but to Annamaria's mind the words fitted Mr. Hazard like a long black cloak.

"Bitter," said Annamaria to herself regretfully, "bitter as gall. And I can remember him when he was the most affectionate, open-hearted boy in the world, with such pretty manners too, and so grateful for the little kindnesses we were able to show him when we lived in the Vale of Health."

"Hazard," said Mr. Hartleigh to his friend, "I think you ought to go back to Spain; the climate of England does not suit you at all. It never did, my dear fellow."

Mr. Hazard glanced at Mr. Hartleigh with a quick suspicion that he was being impertinent. An affectionate, open-hearted boy would never have harboured this suspicion for an instant, but perhaps while Mr. Hazard's hair had been changing from bronze into silver, the virgin gold of his heart had been mixed with a sad alloy. If a heart is open, iron may very easily enter it, to alter the first purity of its metal.

But even the new Mr. Hazard, whose heart was sealed and seared with fire, could not long suspect Mr. Hartleigh of impertinence. The looming eyes were shabby brown velvet like a pair of bat's-wings. They were too soft for Mr. Hazard's irritable taste; too kind by half, he called them to himself, yet not so kind as Mr. Hartleigh. Mr. Hazard answered him politely, but his voice was a plucked fiddlestring of impatience.

"I cannot go back to Spain," said Mr. Hazard, "until I have seen certain people whom I hope to meet in England."

Both Annamaria and Mr. Hartleigh jumped to the comfortable conclusion that he meant his father and sisters, and even possibly his daughter. His other daughter was dead, of course; dead long since, in a vanished September, and the eldest boy, the one whom his father had taken, was dead of a decline these seven years. The second boy, he who had been so dear to Mr. Hazard, had lain quietly in his grave for so long that only Mr. Hazard remembered that he would have been seventeen years old had he lived. So, since his wife and Lionel were in San Sebastian, and since he had already seen Mr. Piggott and Mr. Bird, Annamaria and Hartleigh fell back on the soft cushioned thought that Mr. Hazard must mean his father, and thence were lulled to a dream of reconciliation and filial joy.

In spite of the sound but inexpensive port

now warming their vitals, their hearts would have withered in their bosoms with pure horror had they suspected the truth. Mr. Hazard had no hope of meeting his father, or even the most broad-minded of his sisters. It was precisely these same dead children whom Mr. Hazard so improbably hoped to meet before leaving England.

Not all the port and brandy in Annamaria's best cut-glass decanters could have removed the chill from their hearts could they have seen this hope within the secret mind of Mr. Hazard. But, even supposing that his mind had suddenly become transparent to their eyes, they would certainly have been so dazzled and amazed that this flying hope must have escaped them. Against the interwoven and concentric circles of his thought, against the colours of fire and crystal which informed its moons and stars, they would surely in their amazement have mistaken this hope for a darting bird or a dead leaf. It must have escaped them, even as it escaped them now in Mr. Hazard's few and casual words.

Deliberately he veiled his eyes against their wonder; he did not speak again for several long minutes. Annamaria was annoyed; she had taken a great deal of pains with the dinner, and had gone to the trouble of making the trifle herself. Mr. Hazard had eaten nothing to speak of, but that was no reason why he should not speak at all. He might have spoken about politics or literature, or the green April leaves waving like seaweed in the pool of the evening sky.

"Then you had better have a month in the country," said Mr. Hartleigh; he said it as he might have said: "Then you had better have some hot whisky and water," and indeed he thought of the country as a medicinal tonic rather than a spring of natural delight, for he was a true Cockney.

"I shall need a month, or even two months," said Mr. Hazard carelessly; he did not trouble to conceal his secret plan, for he knew that the influenza had done it for him. No one could possibly suspect Mr. Hazard of going to the country to chase wild geese or ghostly swans while he remained so excessively thin. To anyone with an ounce of common sense it must appear that Mr. Hazard was going to the country to eat butter and eggs, or new green peas and ducklings.

"The seaside, I suppose?" asked Annamaria, with kindly interest. "You wouldn't like Brighton?"

"No," said Mr. Hazard; the exquisite finality of the word was like a soundless charge of gunpowder to demolish the sea-front and lay the pavilion in ruins.

"The true pastoral country will be your best restorative," said Mr. Hartleigh. "The valleys and the verdant hills, the apple blossoms and the lilacs." Mr. Hartleigh saw no reason why a medicinal tonic should not be flavoured with honey and the extracted juice of flowers.

"Doubtless," said Mr. Hazard; courtesy drove him to a dissyllable, but he would have preferred a shorter word, or, better still, to be silent. It was too much trouble to unravel the spliced ends of the nerves which bound his body to his brain, but he was either very much bored or very much wearied by the Hartleighs' conversation. Already his laziness was cracking almonds instead of walnuts for the children, and now he began to make a neat and idle list of words of one syllable which might be employed in decent society. "Yes"; "no"; "quite"; "ah"; "oh"; "still" (this might be cleverly prolonged); "well" (the same rule applied); "thanks" (that was slightly vulgar); "so" (that was Germanic); "good" (excellent); "but" (French and affected; a shrug was implicit). Really, reflected Mr. Hazard above the litter of papery almond shells upon his plate, it was disgraceful, his native tongue's poverty in those polite monosyllables which may save the weariest breath to cool the bitterest porridge.

The room was a cube of hot bright air, moored fast among the thinner airs of twilight. It did not float, as the trees' branches floated and waved visibly in the green element above them, a sky like a lake reversed, grained and patterned like the surface of water, crossed by cool streams of radiance from the west. The room lay heavy and immovable like a drowned hulk at the bottom of this pool of ether; it did not hang suspended like the tree-tops, it was hopelessly weighed down by the soft imponderable air. It lay like a sunken ship, solid, painted with shining phosphorescence. The evening, so light over the tree-tops, was heavy enough to press upon the room, to crush its thick bright atmosphere closer and closer upon

Mr. Hazard's mind. The flame of the lamp and the more gaseous flame of the fire, the dust spangling the bars of brightness with innumerable golden motes, these were emanations too difficult to breathe, too hot and dense for the delicate rhythm of breathing. Mr. Hazard thought how pleasant it would be if only he might be allowed to lift the black marble clock from the mantelpiece and hurl it through the shut window. The glittering splinters of glass would be neither so thin nor so sharp as the April air rushing in through the broken pane. Of course even to open the window in the old-fashioned way would be better than nothing, but Annamaria would be sure to shut it again. She would remind Mr. Hazard that he ought to be careful; she would pull the shawl about her shoulders and talk about toothache.

"I'll write to you, Hartleigh," said Mr. Hazard. "I'll send you an address when I write. Annamaria, I do not know how to thank you for your kindness. . . ."

10

'Tis True 'tis Pity

WHEN Mr. Hazard descended the narrow stairs of the Hartleighs' house in Marylebone upon the last night of April 1833 he stepped from a confined and breathless atmosphere into a fresh green twilight made chill and wholesome by increasing wind. The currents of air were electric with purpose, and the leaves snapped in the wind like little flags and crackled with cold fire overhead. It was an evening for love or the more severe resolves of ambition; as the breeze lifted the hair from Mr. Hazard's tense contracted forehead, it seemed to lift his heart also, though a moment before his heart had been heavier than a stone.

Now, if ever, was the moment for Mr. Hazard to declare himself a free spirit and a saviour of his kind. Such he had indeed set forth to be, and this with greater energy and impatience than remained in him tonight as he laid his hand upon Hartleigh's front door knob. A hundred fitful and intemperate schemes had flourished and died down within the past twenty years, whose fruits were to benefit the race of man from Niagara to the Straits of Propontis, so many exotics sprung from the fertile soil of Mr. Hazard's brain. His brain had yielded far too many of these harvests; nothing remained of them but chaff and worthless straw. Yet they had cost Mr. Hazard quite as dear as if they had been neatly stored in political granaries, safe from the teeth of rodents, locked away as accomplished laws. The four winds had taken his efforts and scattered them nobody knew where.

Tonight one wind was sufficient to blow an illusion of hope across his brain; it is sad to admit that this hope was concerned with nothing more important than his private happiness. Tonight his opportunity lay before him, had he possessed the strength to seize it, brighter and wider than the dingy street which filled his actual field of vision. Now he had the chance of stepping down four steps into the street, and with that descent entering the England of the time, and setting his thin shoulder to some useful revolution of a wheel in the machine. He did not choose to seize this chance; his fatigue and his indifference persuaded him that all such labours were in vain. He knew that his reputation, his character, his very name, were catchwords of conflict and failure; his physical exhaustion prevented him from knowing more, or desiring to know it.

Perhaps if someone had blown a charge upon a key-bugle or chromatic trumpet within Mr. Hazard's hearing at that moment, or had forced him to swallow one-twentieth part of a grain of strychnine or six-pennyworth of common brandy, his energies might have been so far recruited as to drive him into unselfish action. Things being as they were, and the street empty, and he tired and stifled by the Hartleighs' conversation, he had no mind except for his private affairs. Strangely and deplorably, these affairs seemed to him of the highest concern. He went down three steps into the street and paused; the influenza had left his body good for nothing more difficult than a night's sleep, but he might have set his mind to some firm and noble purpose. It is sad to record that he did nothing of the sort; he determined to do exactly as he pleased. He looked from side to side, pleased to be alone and to mature his selfish plans in solitude.

He paused, somewhat giddy from his quick descent of the stairs; he closed his eyes for one moment, but in that wink of darkness he had closed his eyes upon the whole world, upon the four remaining months of spring and summer, upon the turmoil of the public heart and the spirit of the time. He was going into the country to mind his own affairs; he was easily spared from the world and its destinies. The world would go round the sun as smoothly and as swiftly without the help of his affection; it could not be hastened or retarded by his pains. Therefore he was wise to leave it, and to live or die as he pleased.

Fortunately for the world, Mr. Hazard's contemporaries were more diligent than he; not one of them was to waste the long, sweet summer as he had determined to waste it. Southey and Lord Ashley were carrying on a correspondence about factory legislation; the first Reform Parliament had lately assembled, Buxton was taking up the work of Wilberforce, Althorpe was amending the poor-laws, and Roebuck bringing forward a vast new scheme of education. Lord John Russell was asking Thomas Moore to go to Ireland with him;

"Your being a rebel may somewhat atone for my being a cabinet minister," said Lord John Russell, but Thomas Moore could not go to Ireland after all, because he, poor fellow, had promised to write lives of the literati for Dr. Lardner's *Cabinet Cyclopædia.* Wordsworth was worried about the realm, but delighted with his first grandchild; he was planning a walking tour in Scotland with Crabb Robinson as a holiday, but he would not stop composing Evening Voluntaries while he walked.

Mr. Macaulay was writing to his sister from the smoking-room of the House of Commons; in June he would be happy to inform her that in less than a fortnight he would dine with Lord Grey, Mr. Boddington, Mr. Price, Sir Robert Inglis, Lord Ripon, and Lord Morpeth. Everyone was busy and devoted. Young Mr. Whiteley was finishing his pamphlet "Three Months in Jamaica," and the Anti-Slavery Society was awaiting it with eagerness. Wilberforce was dying, and Haydon was painting the Reform Banquet and hearing plenty of excellent stories while he painted. Sometimes these tales were tragic; Sir Charles Bagot told him that Michelangelo's copy of Dante, with a wide margin and his own designs, fell into the hands of the Bishop of Derry and was lost on the passage to Marseilles. There were quantities of new books to offset such losses; Mr. Tennyson's exquisite lyrics, Mr. Browning's *Pauline*, Hartley Coleridge's poems.

Everyone was active for the future. Mr. Landor was preparing to plant thirteen hundred vines at Fiesole, and forty fruit-trees. Lord Nugent was upon the point of sailing for the Ionian Isles. The Oxford Movement was to be set in startling motion by Keble's sermon at Saint Mary's. Mr. Hallam was to die in Vienna, and Mr. Tennyson was to begin writing *In Memoriam*.

Everyone was very energetic. The Greek Islands were in revolt. Hussein Pasha had just left Constantinople for the front, and in the third week in May the ban of outlawry would be launched against Mehemet Ali. A few days later Ibrahim was to break down the gates of Gaza and storm the city of Acre. Upon the eighth of July, the eleventh anniversary of Mr. Shelley's death by drowning, a treaty was to be signed in the palace of Unkiar Skelessi. Meanwhile Mr. Gordon's

History of the Greek Revolution would be published in London without a single reference to the unfortunate Mr. Hazard.

In France people were having their own adventures. Grisi had pleased the carping Parisian taste as Semiramide. George Sand had met Alfred de Musset at a dinner given by the *Revue des deux mondes;* already they were planning picnics at Fontainebleau; by September they would be *en route* for Venice. Amelia Opie gave tea-parties in the Hôtel de la Paix, wearing a lawn cap with whimpers and crimped frills.

In England everyone was sedulous and earnest. Haydon, going to visit the graves of his children in Paddington New Churchyard, perceived that the name on Mrs. Siddons's headstone was almost obliterated; Malibran was playing at Drury Lane to the enchantment of thousands. After repeated applications the act was finally obtained permitting the extension of the Liverpool and Manchester Railway as far south as Birmingham. Mr. Cobbett had stopped riding about the country, but not before Mr. Trevor had been pelted out of Sunderland with rotten potatoes.

Not everyone was lucky, but nearly everyone was industrious. Poor Mrs. Hemans had left her pretty "Dove's Nest" above Windermere and gone to live with her brother in Dublin; she had just sent Dora Wordsworth *The Remains of Lucretia Davidson.* The Wordsworths missed her sadly, but were glad that even in idle Ireland she found time to work.

A few people were very unlucky, but nobody was lazy except Mr. Hazard. He had suffered a severe attack of influenza, but this was not sufficient reason for the complete prostration of his powers of will. If he felt incapable of returning to Greece, he might at least have gone to Limerick, to dissuade Gerald Griffin from joining the Society of Christian Brothers; he might have interested himself in the pathetic fate of John Clare. Mrs. Emmerson had given John Clare a cow, to be called by the charming name of Blossom or May; his cottage at Northborough was thatched, and covered with climbing roses. Nevertheless he was beginning to be haunted by evil spirits; Mr. Hazard, who was familiar with all spirits, might have helped him to exorcise these.

Even the women were working hard this summer; little Miss Landon was particularly hardworking, in her attic room at 22 Hans Place. Although the poor child lived circumspectly, as a boarder in the school establishment of the Misses Lance, she was pursued by cruel slanders; perhaps she was too young and too pretty to escape them save by an incautious dose of prussic acid. Mrs. Norton was busy with the *New Monthly*, and *Friendship's Offering*, and *The Keepsake*, and Mr. Norton was being detestable. Mrs. Shelley had made a sacrifice for Percy in leaving London and going to live at Harrow; she had begun *Lodore*, and undertaken a series of lives of the Italian literati for Dr. Lardner. Hogg's *Shelley Papers* had appeared in the *New Monthly Magazine;* Medwin had written a small volume of *Shelley Papers*. Mary was beginning to believe that she might attempt another edition of the poems, but she knew that Sir Timothy would never consent to a memoir. Leigh Hunt had published *The Masque of Anarchy*, with a preface.

Everyone was changing houses and opinions; Leigh Hunt had gone to Chelsea, and Trelawney had gone to America. When Lady Morgan went to France, her little black harp case was mistaken for a *petit mort* upon its last journey to Père Lachaise.

Coleridge was comfortable in the Gillmans' house at Highgate, but not everyone was so comfortable as Coleridge. Charles Lamb and his sister were living at Bay Cottage, Enfield, a mournful yellow house kept by a woman called Redford. It was believed that this atrocious person locked Miss Lamb in a dark cupboard as a punishment for cutting up a feather-bed and scattering the feathers out of window. Mr. Hazard was to be congratulated upon the superior patience of Mrs. Downing, for his conduct must often have been difficult for even the kindest landlady to understand. He never cut his mattress into pieces, but he frequently spent the night upon the hearth-rug when he did not spend it upon Hampstead Heath. If he had not paid his bills with such regularity, Mrs. Downing would have been glad to know that Mr. Hazard was going into the country to mind his own business and forget the progress of civilization.

II

Ere Babylon Was Dust

HE stood upon the pavement and drank the thin sharp air; it flowed about his head in a cool stream of felicity. He thought that if he followed it to its source, as if it were a true river, it might lead him wherever he desired to go. It seemed scarcely worth the pains of piecing the ragged map of his plan together if he followed this river of air to its source, which must be a spring of light among leaves far greener than these London leaves, on which a little soot already lay in flakes of black velvet.

If Mr. Hazard had eaten more mutton for dinner, or even a few of the macaroons in Annamaria's trifle, he might not so readily have believed that a river of air may be traced to its source, or that the source, once found, will reveal itself as a fountain of light. Out of the dark and odious pit of depression into which the powers of weariness had cast him his released soul sped like an arrow to a mark which his own mind had that instant traced upon the future. He had not the least doubt of the veracity of this vision. He did not know that his own mind, unreasonably swift and impetuous, had fled away in front of his wishes and struck the fountain of light from the blank rocky wall of the future. But he saw the light in the distance much more plainly than the dim brassy number above Mrs. Downing's door.

"I shall go there in the morning; early in the morning," said Mr. Hazard to himself as he climbed the stair. He pulled off his black jacket and his narrow black waistcoat with the steel buttons, and without waiting a moment beyond the flash of a tinder-box and the leap of a candle flame, he began to throw his white shirts and his attenuated black trousers and his brown and gilded and vermilion books into the largest of his three boxes. He thought of nothing save the ecstasy of haste; he worked like a happy madman, like a slave driven by beatitude. When he caught a swift image of himself in the glass, he was far too profoundly enchanted by hurry to notice that he no longer wore a stretched and brittle mask of pride over a thin skull-face detestable in its own sight. He recognized the face, in rapid passing, as one he had known before, and casually accepted as a friend's. It was, thanks to the illumination of a baseless hope and the light of a single candle, almost precisely the same face, flushed, excited, bright-eyed, baffled, triumphant, intent upon a secret purpose, which he had been used to see glancing at him from behind the dark glass of a damp-spotted mirror some twenty years before.

The delicious useless violence of haste warmed more than Mr. Hazard's heart; his brow streamed with salty sweat, which ran into his eyes and twisted his hair into curlicues of silver. The clear green sky was darkened by a slanting tidal wave of rain; the rain beat wildly at the windows, and Mr. Hazard opened both the windows and let the rain drive in, along the dusty carpet, along the tops of the tables, with a prodigious sound of blown foolscap paper and the fluttering open leaves of books. The books and papers were spattered with rain as Mr. Hazard tumbled them helter-skelter into the boxes, and presently there was a bright pool of rain-water under the windows. The candle flared into a small pillar of fire and died in the wind, but there still remained enough pale and aqueous light within the room to permit Mr. Hazard to throw his books into the boxes, among a tangle of luminous white shirts and attenuated black trousers.

The white shirt that he wore was soaked with rain and sweat; he pulled it over his head and worked stripped to the waist in a cool whirlpool of wind and rain. He hitched his long trousers tighter about his waist, and the private wind of his own speed was added to the April wind from without. With a cutlass between his teeth and a handful of ingots among the gilded books he might have been a gentleman-pirate flinging Peru and India into triple sea-chests. His plan was patched together as he worked; he flew upon its quick previsions, lifted above all weariness and doubt, refreshed and medicined by certainty. He felt the cool sweat of his own body washed by the cooler stream of rain; after he had corded the boxes, he stood by the open window and let the storm sweep over him in waves of pure ravishment. He wondered why he had been so foolish as to have nightmares of late; it needed only a little haste and a few millions of clean rain-drops to overcome such monstrous dreams for ever.

Book Two

THE YOUNG HUNTINGS

Book Two

THE YOUNG HUNTINGS

I

Reverie over an Apple-tart

THE next morning, which happened to be the
first of May, came up out of the east like an apple
orchard in full bloom. Mr. Hazard was to travel
westward; he knew that by nightfall he would be
among true orchards of cherry and apple, and
that the sun would go down in a golden forest of
clouds. He was driven betimes to the inn from

which the Gravelow coach set forth; he forgot to drink his tea, he confounded his boxes in a string of Greek oaths thicker than the actual cords which bound them, but at heart he was extremely happy. There was no longer a cracking icicle within his breast; the season's influence had melted it.

The day was fine, the weather was warm and sweet as new bread and honey, yet by eleven o'clock Mr. Hazard was wishing for his greatcoat. He knew he had rolled the clumsy thing into a wrinkled ball and tossed it into one of the boxes, but he was not sure whether it lay under Plato or on top of Lord Nugent's *Memorials of John Hampden*. The coach was stuffy and hot, and Mr. Hazard had pulled off his neckcloth and dropped his hat beneath a pair of muddy boots which did not belong to him. Nevertheless he wished he had been wise enough to wear his greatcoat.

Mr. Hazard's body did not match the breadth of his mind; he had always been tall, but he had never been wide. Therefore he was seldom afforded sufficient room in public and private conveyances; his memory in this matter was accurate to the brink of the cradle. As a child he had been nearly smothered by his mother's shawls and his sister's furbelows; his cousins, his tutors, and his friends had all taken an unfair half of any post-chaise. By forty he had been crushed and pummelled to the conclusion that in a fatted civilization he did well to wear a greatcoat.

The inclemency of winter wrought a natural cure of this injustice; Mr. Hazard was cold; he wore a greatcoat; his greatcoat was old-fashioned and voluminous, and he was falsely credited with the ability to fill its ample folds. In winter Mr. Hazard was frequently allowed breathing-space within a stage-coach. The capes of his greatcoat were deceptive, and very fat people preferred to sit beside timid old ladies in tippets, or poor little shivering boys going to school for the first time. But in summer the secret was out; the skeleton was uncovered. The minute his wife put his great-coat away in camphor Mr. Hazard was at the mercy of the world.

There had been no stage-coaches upon the slopes of Mount Parnassus, and the peasants had often made way for him as he passed with his arm in a sling. In Arabia one could wear a burnous and appear capable of breaking a camel's back. In Spain and Italy the diligences carried a plague of priests, fat priests who battened upon garlic and strong red wine. The thin ones fixed their eyes upon their breviaries and let the populace squeeze them into corners; the fat ones sat down beside Mr. Hazard with complacent grunts. In England it was a secular scourge; the Gravelow coach was crammed with prosperous farmers and their wives and with shopkeepers who were undoubtedly successful. There was a crowd of pleasant young gentlemen on top who were not minded to make room for anyone whose age was over twenty-five and whose weight was under ten stone.

Within the coach Mr. Hazard was given as much indulgence as the least of the baskets and bandboxes. His neighbours regarded his long legs as a public nuisance, and he himself was unaware of the fate of his doubled-up knees amid the welter of top-boots, Bedford cord breeches, gaiters, black silk aprons, and merino petticoats which surrounded them. His smashed ribs, set by an eccentric Greek surgeon in the cave of the chief Odysseus, had never seemed so flimsy and unstable as they did now under the prodding elbows of the shopkeepers. He forgave the shopkeepers, but he was furiously angry with his broken ribs; he ground his teeth and longed to grind the ramshackle bones to graveyard dust.

Mr. Hazard's acute discomfort did not prevent him from being happy; the upper layer of his sensations was like a short and irritable piecrust over a deep and smiling apple-tart. He evolved this unpoetical simile as he ate his dinner in the parlour of the Holtspur at Beaconsfield; he finished his biscuit and cheese and fixed his eyes upon a blossoming enclosure whose tree-tops were tufted with the promise of a thousand apples.

Now his own mind bloomed with auguries; it was spring, the jocund freshness of a morning to which high summer will succeed as noon. The autumnal evening of such a time could not fail to be a harvest of contentment. Only good luck could grow in such a land and such a season. Some devil had sown tares in the garden he had sought to plant in this green valley, but his impatience had despaired too soon; he had let an army of wretched weeds drive him out of his inheritance. He had been infantile in his swift despair; he had never lacked courage, but he had lacked fidelity and that careless trust in his own powers which is worth more to a man than the affection of families and the approval of publics. He should have forgotten his gibbering peers; he should have ignored the brute commonalty. He should have let the world run softly by, as the Thames ran softly between water-meadows, until all his songs were ended.

In Italy, where pulses are reputed to beat quickly, a newly-wedded man will plant a hillside with silver olive saplings, and rest peacefully in the knowledge that not until his grandsons' day will any kin of his pluck profit from those trees. A slow harvest of yellow oil will ripen through the years to anoint the hands of future generations, but the man who planted them will go to his grave long before that treasure is pressed from the fruit of the olive-trees.

"A wise and instructive custom," mused Mr. Hazard, "flourishing in a soil made meagre by superstition and vice. I should have planted apple-trees in the Thames valley; my orcharding would have been in good heart by now."

Some river running softly through the shadowed valleys of his mind had washed them clear of bitterness and self-reproach; they were full of light, even as the low valley of the Thames overflowed with sunset. His mood, which should have been elegiac to suit the hour, preserved the plain simplicity of early morning. He had regained some lost innocence of the spirit; he spoke of planting orchards, but his hopes were as inviolate as though his first parents had never tasted apples.

He called for his bill in Arabic, and paid for his dinner in Spanish gold, but nobody minded these irregularities in the least, since the price of the dinner was three shillings in English currency, and Mr. Hazard did not ask for change.

At Gravelow the wide curving street brimmed with the flood of sunset above the brimming reaches of the Thames. By every rule of logic, by every impulse of sensibility, Mr. Hazard should have been drowned in sorrowful memories. His mood bore him like a strong swimmer across the double streams of light and water, and set him down quite safely in front of a little fire in the coffee-room of the Crown inn. He was not even out of breath; the waves of some mysterious power had laid him to rest in a comfortable arm-chair, and then receded, softly and more softly still, along the infinite conduits of the night.

2

Satan Finds Some Mischief Still

MR. HAZARD knew that he must find lodgings, if only to have a mantelpiece upon which to range his seven Hebrew grammars. The next morning was gay with fickle sunshowers; it was a harlequin day, a strayed reveller from April, in glittering lozenges of blue and silver. Mr. Hazard and the erratic shadow of a cloud trod lightly down the High Street together, a grey shade and a black shade upon a pavement already dappled with rain-drops and disks of brightness.

Mr. Hazard found lodgings without trouble because he refused to take any trouble; it was pure auspicious chance that the lodgings happened to possess plenty of clean window-panes to the east and south, through which the sun shone upon scrubbed paint and chintzes laundered into holes. He paid a week's rent in advance, believed that he would want no dinner, consented to the suggestion of an egg with his tea, and walked swiftly along West Street until he came to the little house where he had once lived. It was precisely as he had left it; he could have made a pencil sketch from memory before he turned the curve of the road. The larger house opposite, which had belonged to Mr. Bird, stood solid and unchanged.

He leaned against the red brick wall in front of this house and gazed at the green front door through which he had emerged so often into the mornings of a younger spring. He had a small precise picture of himself in his mind's eye, exact and critical, etched in sharp lines and bitten with the acid of irony. He laughed shortly under his breath and dismissed his own ghost to oblivion. The ghost of a living man must be a poor creature at best; a stuffless thing, projected into sunshine by a sick brain. But the ghosts of the dead are different; they are sustained and animated by spirits whole and entire, they possess their proper souls. Mr. Hazard watched the green door as though it had been the entrance to a forest glade and he a hunter awaiting with suspended pulses the delicate approach of a troop of wild deer.

The green door remained shut; the forest glade shimmered in the distance, caught in a criss-cross net of light and shade. No foot, however soft and fleeting, disturbed its feathery grass. Not even a solitary fawn fled down the forest glade with shy and subtle steps.

The hunter subdued his breathing and the beating of his heart and waited, his eyes upon the unopening door. Mr. Hazard knew it was in vain; he took the air into his lungs and the knowledge into his heart with a single sigh. This was not the morning for stalking wild deer; he must let them come of their own accord if they came at all.

He returned to his lodgings; he was so tired that he determined not to be idle. The influenza had given him a thirst for doing nothing which parched his mouth and turned his bones to powder, but he refused to slake his thirst in the cool depths of idleness. His luggage had been sent from the inn; he unpacked his boxes with speed and passion, leaving his garments in a heap in the middle of the floor while he arranged his books with extreme care upon the table, the chimney-piece, the chairs, and the shelves of the corner cupboard. The rows collapsed in clouds of dust, like castles builded of mighty cards, and he buttressed them at either end with piles of heavier volumes. Then he stood regarding them affectionately; his thin fingers were covered with London soot, and there was a streak of London soot across his forehead like a dark chrism. He had a wistful desire to read Lucian as a relaxation after his labours, and a passing regret that he had wasted so many guineas on Dyce's edition of Shirley's works. He had bought the books because of Shirley's melancholy end, and because he disliked Dryden.

Conquering these weaknesses, he turned to the seven Hebrew grammars and selected the heaviest with the inevitable instinct of the martyr. From the same shelf he took the King James version of the Holy Bible, the Septuagint, and the Old Testament in the original Hebrew characters. Hastily dropping a few note-books and pencils into his pockets, he put the four thick volumes into a cracked leather knapsack and prepared to leave the room. The knapsack was slung over his shoulder, his foot was on the threshold, he had almost bumped his head against the lintel of the door, when he hesitated, wavered, and returned.

With a slightly guilty nonchalance he picked up his worn copy of *Paradise Lost* from the table and thrust it into his pocket among the pencils. Then he ran downstairs as if his cracked knapsack were a pair of wings.

"I must get on with it," thought Mr. Hazard, who was longing for the company of Satan and feeling abominably lazy about Job. He had always meant to write a poetic drama with Job for its hero; he felt that his own experiences had fitted him with acquired talents for the task. As a matter of fact, he had written the first act, with its magnificent lamenting strophe and antistrophe, during the confusion of Lionel's Christmas holidays. Mr. Hazard was aware that the spiritual agony crying from his verse would have drawn blood from brutal adamant, but he was not quite content with the language.

It was noble; it was musical; it was tranced and ecstatic with sorrow. But was it better than the vulgar tongue of the prose version that certain anonymous gentlemen had dedicated to King James?

Mr. Hazard had decided to make his own translation. He did not trust the Greek, and so there was nothing for it but to turn the Hebrew straight into what the true lovers of his poetry were already beginning to call Hazardous English. This meant that Mr. Hazard must learn Hebrew, but the learning of Hebrew meant very little to Mr. Hazard, who had learnt Sanscrit and Chinese and the first thirteen letters of the Pali alphabet. He had begun his studies upon New Year's Eve, while Lionel was singing a Spanish carol, and at the end of four months he was proficient enough to answer Bildad and Zophar and Eliphaz and to argue eloquently with the Lord in his own language.

"I must get on with it," thought Mr. Hazard for the second time; he was so tired that he felt a fanatical horror of idleness. If he slipped into the cool depths of idleness, he might so easily forget about Job and fall asleep for ever.

"I shall walk to Medmenham Abbey,"

thought Mr. Hazard, "and I shall do the thirty-eighth chapter, with the Lord challenging Job from the whirlwind."

It is a singular instance of the folly of man's proposals that ten minutes later Mr. Hazard found himself in a light skiff with a pair of oars in his hands. The knapsack lay behind him unopened, but the copy of *Paradise Lost* was placed carefully upon the opposite seat, as if Mr. Hazard found Satan a more congenial vis-à-vis than Job. Twenty years of reading him had given Mr. Hazard Satan by heart; sometimes he regarded him as a beloved friend, but more often he identified the fallen angel with himself. It was the profoundest idleness to read Milton, for the words welled into his mind from his deeper memory; they were become a part of his mind, and to read them over was like murmuring a prayer learned in childhood, save that the words were not a prayer but a defiance.

The sound of the river, and its scent, and its cool colour, flowed past him in a dream; it was the distilled essence of idleness, the very element of peace. Upon its lifted banks the beech-trees were thin green flames that burned above the oaks.

"I shall row until I am tired," thought Mr. Hazard, who was already tired, "and then I shall find a quiet backwater where nothing can possibly come to bother me. Perhaps, after all, I deserve a little peace and quiet. 'Is my strength the strength of stones, or is my flesh of brass?' I shall go to sleep in a backwater and nothing shall worry me for the rest of the day."

3

Sunshine Holy-day

"EXCUSE me, but would you very much mind waking up and giving me back my silver arrow? I can't shoot properly with any of the others."

The voice, which was sufficiently sweet, but high and chirping like a bird's, reached Mr. Hazard after a brief interval; it fell into the resounding cavern of his dream and waked him without a start. It did not fall suddenly; it drifted lightly down, it descended like a shuttlecock buoyed up by air, and touched him no more heavily than a feather or a leaf.

He did not move or even open his eyes; he

lay supine in the hollow well of his dream. He was aware of no reason why he should answer the voice; if he had ever stolen silver arrows, that was in another life, upon another planet. He lay without speaking until someone spoke for him.

"It's rather ridiculous to ask the poor man to give you back your silver arrow, as if he were a thief and had taken it on purpose. Why don't you explain to him politely that you're a wretched shot and that it's sticking in his left shoulder instead of in the target?"

The other voice was a second shuttlecock, made of softer feathers; it was neither so merry nor so sharp as the first voice. Mr. Hazard wondered if it told the truth; without opening his eyes, he moved his hand until it brushed against a feathered shaft sprouting from his left shoulder. It was a curious circumstance; in his youth he might have called it miraculous. Even today, when he had meant to bother about nothing under heaven, he was tempted to look into this matter of the silver arrow.

He opened his eyes; he looked up, and at first he saw nothing but a dazzle of sunlight among translucent leaves like tongues of fire. Then, as the prismatic colours shifted and grew still, he saw the figures of two girls leaning from the bank above him. He saw them through the blindness of his dream, girls like trees dancing, like little birches turning the river-bank into a frieze.

"But would you mind giving it to me, whether I'm a bad shot or not?" said the chirping voice of one.

"He's asleep," said the other. "If you crawled along that branch and bent down, you might just manage to reach it, Allegra."

"But how silly to say he's asleep! His eyes are wide open."

Mr. Hazard's eyes were indeed wide open; he had not known that anyone was named Allegra nowadays. The music of the three familiar syllables was confused by echoes.

"That isn't really your name, is it?" asked Mr. Hazard with that slight impatient movement of the lips which he still believed to be a smile.

"Why shouldn't it be my name? Of course it is; I was named after a rich great-aunt. But give me my arrow, will you please? We're in a hurry." The voice of Allegra had a sweet scolding note in it, like a bird's.

"People are always surprised," said the softer voice. "It isn't really a great-aunt's name; we were named for poems, or something, because we weren't boys. I think it's rather a shame. I'm Rosa; Penserosa, you see."

"Is your mother fond of Milton?" asked Mr. Hazard, who had always wanted to meet a mother who was fond of Milton.

"No, of course not; she isn't in the least fond of him, and neither are we. It was a bet, I think; someone bet my father that we wouldn't be boys, and we weren't. The boys, you see, are always Tristram and Hilary. This detestable man thought it would be clever to invent the same sort of names for us; wasn't it horrid of him?"

Mr. Hazard sat up in the skiff and looked at the two girls; their heads were like preposterous and lovely flowers grafted upon the willow boughs. He thought them the prettiest children he had ever seen.

"The detestable man made rather a brilliant

guess," he said. "How old were you when you were christened, and suppose he'd named you the other way round?"

"Yes, that's quite true," said Rosa. "But that makes it a little bit dull, having our names match our natures. The boys have come out wrong, which is much more amusing. Tristram's an agreeable rattle, and Hilary's as solemn as an owl."

"May I have my silver arrow, please?" asked Allegra for the fourth time, like an angry bird.

"Of course; I'm so sorry," said Mr. Hazard. He plucked the arrow from his shoulder; it had pierced his linen shirt without touching him. It was a queer plaything, with a silver varnished shaft and a blue feather.

Mr. Hazard stood up in the skiff and gave the arrow to Allegra. He thought her the most beautiful creature he had ever seen.

4

Clairvoyant

PRECISELY why he thought this will never be known. Perhaps she slipped, like molten crystal, into some mould which his imagination had prepared since childhood; perhaps her changeling grace was sister to some necessity of his heart. Allegra was lovely, but Rosa was lovely as Allegra; Rosa was warmer, sweeter, and more pensive, softened by small compunctions and pities. They were twins in delicate flesh and bone, but barely kindred in their varying colours and in the light and darkness of their hair. Rosa was serious, and Mr. Hazard adored a contemplative brow banded with shadowy tresses; she was gentle, and Mr. Hazard was happiest in gentle presences. Nevertheless he chose the silver rather than the gold, the moon rather than the sun, the water rather than the fire, the sharp flower of the snow-flake rather than the tender flower of the earth.

Having chosen, he allowed his eyes the brief refreshment of another glance; his eyes, perpetually wearied by Hebrew grammars, were comforted by Allegra's cool regard. He was a beholder in whose eyes beauty dwelt at all times to enchant the visible world, but in this moment he was neither dazzled nor blinded; he saw the sprightly imperfections, the exquisite flaws in this being compact of grace and mockery, and he would not have altered her by the length of an eyelash or the smoothing of a hair.

"Thank you," said Allegra, taking the arrow with a smile, half of politeness and half of pleased amusement. Mr. Hazard looked so very odd in Allegra's cool blue eyes that she could not keep her pink mouth from turning up at the corners. Allegra was cheerfully practical; she wanted to laugh, and she also wanted to set Mr. Hazard among the strawberry beds to scare away the birds. In Allegra's merry and intolerant judgment Mr. Hazard would make an admirable scarecrow; as a man he was ridiculous.

Rosa's more charitable mind transmuted this opinion into a belief that Mr. Hazard might possibly be poor and that he must certainly be hungry. The ingenious goodness of her heart sought for some means of providing him with the wing of a chicken and a large slice of plum-cake. There was a red and green basket under the willow-trees, and several stone bottles of ginger-beer.

"Have you come far this afternoon?" asked Rosa. "Oh, I see; from Gravelow. And are you going back in time for dinner?"

"No," said Mr. Hazard, "I have my dinner with me." He picked up his coat and looked in all the pockets; he was sure he had put some bread and cheese into his pocket before he left his lodgings.

"So have we," said Rosa, "in that basket; it's nice eating one's dinner out of doors, isn't it?" She smiled, but she was very sorry for Mr. Hazard, because he couldn't find his bread and cheese.

"Do have some of ours," she said when she could bear it no longer; Mr. Hazard had found at least twenty pencils and a number of old letters, but not a single crumb of bread and cheese.

Allegra looked at Rosa, raising her arched eyebrows into light satiric wings above her amazement. Her small lips formed soundless words in the still air.

"Mama wouldn't let us," she breathed, inaudibly save to her sister's accustomed senses. "She wouldn't like his rowing up the backwater; I think she'd say he was a tramp."

Mr. Hazard was holding his coat upsidedown and shaking it, and watching the pencils fall into the bottom of the skiff. His sensitive perceptions were distracted by his search; he failed to catch even the faintest whisper of Allegra's words. Had he heard them, nothing could have prevented him from racing back to Gravelow like a proud and somewhat ragged flash of lightning but he did not hear them, and he remained among the willows of the backwater, at the mercy of a sportive and capricious fate.

"That's absurd," said Rosa aloud. Mr. Hazard thought she meant his own behaviour; he accepted the comment with a laugh.

"It is, of course," he said, "I seem to have forgotten my dinner; sometimes I do. It doesn't matter in the least, as I don't happen to be hungry."

"You must be hungry; you've been rowing," said Rosa firmly; privately she thought he must have starved in an Irish famine, or been locked in an underground dungeon upon a diet of bread and water. Rosa was less practical than Allegra; she read romances and even occasionally poetry. But she was practical enough to open the basket and to give Mr. Hazard the wing of a chicken and three slices of brown bread and butter.

He sat in the skiff and the children sat upon the river-bank under the shadow of the willows.

There were no apple blossoms to be seen, but the wind had lately blown over an orchard; it scattered invisible petals upon the surface of the water. The armour of a dragon-fly shone like a driftwood flame.

Mr. Hazard was happy, happy as a hunter who watches a forest glade down which a troop of deer approach with shy and subtle steps. He looked at Allegra, and through the bright crystal of Allegra's face he perceived the vague and faintly tinted faces of other children, lovely, but no lovelier than Allegra, and perhaps, now that Allegra smiled at him, no dearer to his heart. He was content to have it so; to gaze into the clear, sharply faceted crystal of Allegra's face and to see therein the tragic past and the tired present and the austere future, melted into a single beam of light.

5

Capture of a Black Sheep

LADY CLARA HUNTING was the youngest and by far the prettiest daughter of that Lord Camphile who had been Poynyard of the East India Company, and who had died the Earl of Camphile and Eden. It may be remembered by people who take an interest in such matters that Gerald Poynyard had the misfortune to lose his first wife; she perished in Persia under distressing circumstances, leaving Gerald a widower at the age of twenty-eight. Jennifer Poynyard had never been robust, either in body or soul; her strange Arcadian beauty perished with her, as she left no child, and little recollection of herself save in the grief of her parents and in Gerald's passing regret.

At the time he was Poynyard of India; he was far too deeply occupied by affairs of state to be melancholy except upon the rare occasions when he dined alone, and even then he found a good French novel a very fair substitute for a silent wife. He returned to England at the end of ten years, and remarried almost immediately, choosing a beautiful and well-bred girl from the outer branches of one of the great Whig houses. Augusta's beauty was not so pure and rarefied as Jennifer's, but her mind was strong and her stamina excellent. It would be untrue to say that she was never afraid of Gerald, but she hid her fear under her arrogant good looks and her composed and agreeable manner. She was witty; quite witty enough for Gerald, whose superior wit was contemptuous of gifts he could so easily outmatch. He was fond of her; he thought her handsome and healthy, if a little too self-assured. He was severely unaware of her talkative moods, and when her *jeux d'esprit* jarred upon his sensibilities, he philosophically thanked his stars that he had not after all married that minx Rosalba Berni, whom he had met at M. Voltaire's. Wit was a confounded nuisance with one's first cup of tea.

Augusta bore him three pretty little girls in rapid succession; Gerald was courteous, and often commented upon his daughters' comeliness, but although he appeared attached to Geraldine and tolerant of Sophia, he was distinctly annoyed by Clara's advent. His wife's friends were vastly relieved when her fourth child indulgently decided to be a boy.

Although named for his maternal grandfather, Charles Augustine was so precisely like Gerald that his mother found it impossible to make friends with him. If the thing had not been unthinkable, she might sometimes have thought that it was impossible to be fond of him. He was a brilliant and self-possessed child, and his father's features were so perfectly reproduced in miniature upon his small pale face that one might almost have believed that the Mexican savages had stolen Gerald's head and shrunk it up with red-hot sand into the minute proportions of a baby's skull.

Augustine was sent to school at the age of five; Gerald was even more Spartan with his children than with himself. In that same autumn Augusta took her girls to Paris, explaining politely that she disapproved of convents, and that if the poor children were to learn French properly, they must live in France. She had been extremely frivolous in a stately way of her own, yet she relinquished the prospect of London gaieties without a sigh, and her large grey eyes were luminous with relief as she gave her husband an affectionate farewell kiss.

Augusta and the three little girls grew calm and rosy during their first month in Paris; from being anæmic and nervous they bloomed into liveliness and dimples. From that time onward they were always pink and sweetly cheerful; their

French was faultless, their complexions exquisite. It was no wonder that when Augusta brought them out in London, everyone fell in love with their ringlets and their laughter. It was their care-free laughter, even more than their irregular verbs, that their mother had sought to cultivate in the sunny seclusion of the faubourg Saint-Germain.

It had become a habit with them which Gerald had to accept whether he liked it or not. He liked it well enough when they laughed their way into three suitable matches, of which his favourite Geraldine's was inevitably the best. Lord Camphile's fortune was enormous, but he wanted it all for Augustine; his provision for his girls was comparatively modest, and he was rather proud of them for having contrived to marry themselves off so cleverly. Clara had not been so clever as the others, but he had never cared for Clara. Her mother adored her, a mere indulgence of self-love, for she was her mother over again in finer porcelain, turned on a lighter wheel and touched with brighter dyes. Her beauty was a flattering mirror to Augusta's face.

This was the lady whom Allegra called

Mama, who now came down a narrow path among the willow-trees. Clara was three-and-thirty at this time, only seven years younger than Mr. Hazard, but no one seeing them together would have credited the calendar fact. Clara's fair hair, flaxen at twenty, was now pale chestnut quite unmarred by grey; her long-lashed eyes were dark and transparent as amethysts. Her skin, white as Allegra's, lacked the freckles which the sun had sprinkled like golden sequins on Allegra's little nose and smooth ingenuous brow. Clara was prettier than her daughters, more elegant and more composed. Her youthful laughter was now softened and diffused into a thousand slight enchanting smiles; the quality of her charm was evanescent, but although it appeared for ever fleeing, it filled the air about her like a perfume. Mr. Hazard watched her unhurried smooth approach with sentiments of pleasure; her gliding step, her gown of thin blue muslin, even the tinted cameo at her throat, seemed emblematical of peace. Mr. Hazard trusted such a lady to be kind as he would have trusted a cluster of white grapes to be sweet or a moss rose to be fragrant.

She looked at her daughters with a question-ing smile which was nevertheless quick and in-sistent; her eyebrows elevated themselves into the waves of her hair and she waited, dubious and amused. Mr. Hazard, who had risen, made a long step to the river-bank, and Rosa spoke.

"We've forgotten to ask you your name . . . " said Rosa apologetically, blushing under her mother's scrutiny, which suspended judgment and forebore to scold as yet.

"Hazard," said Mr. Hazard. Suddenly he despaired; reality overwhelmed him like a muddy tide. He swallowed mud; he breathed a suffocat-ing darkness; he knew that the sound of his name would break the tranquil surface of the scene, and drown him in humiliation. He leaned against a tree, faint with the apprehended stroke.

It did not fall. It hovered about his head, and slid into the grasses at his feet as harmlessly as a deflected lightning flash. In the vibrating balance of Clara's mind, curiosity weighed more heavily than horror, and she smiled again.

"Then you're the Mr. Hazard who . . ." said Clara against her well-bred will, and straightway poured a warm balsam of words into the freezing pause that gaped between them like a wound.

It was all true; Clara made it seem even truer. They had met in Venice, soon after Mr. Hazard had returned from Greece with his arm in a becoming black silk scarf. Everyone knew that the chieftains had tried to make Mr. Hazard King of Greece, and so several people in Venice had asked him to tea. Mr. Hazard had refused all the invitations except one; his wife had wept because he refused; and he had gone with her to a palace near the Church of Saint John and Saint Paul, and sat for half an hour in a hot room full of candlelight and tuberoses and the tinkle of women's voices. Clara remembered his white face and the dazed brilliance of his eyes, whose glances moved up and down the long, crowded room seeking for a ladder of escape above the roofs, for a stairway sunk into the bottom of the lagoons. While she ate a strawberry sherbet, she had decided that he was a fool rather than a fiend.

He had changed a little in seven years; the silver of his hair was startling against the parchment colour of his face. The dazed brilliance of

his glance moved up and down the river, seeking
for a channel of escape.

Clara felt inquisitive and sorry; she wondered
very much whether the wicked Mr. Hazard were
not belied by his silvery wolf's clothing. She knew
how easily her evasive smiles could charm him
even if he were a wolf. But of course he was only
another black sheep; the thorns and briars of the
reasonable world were tagged with locks of vision-
ary wool from the fleece of such poor creatures.

6

Three Ladies in Haloes

THE makeshift armour contrived by Mr. Hazard's
pride was doubled by a horrid lining; it might have
been woven from nettles or horsehair and steeped
in the blood of the dying centaur. It was, however, quite invisible; only its disastrous effect
upon his nerves could be conjectured by Clara's
bland judicious gaze. Her quick intelligence, un-
dulled by excessive education, her perceptive
sympathies, which rarely involved her heart, her
experience, which swept lightly over humanity,
bright and shallow as a summer rainfall, these

qualities enabled her to look into the depths of Mr. Hazard's mind with a gracious ceremonial smile. If she had looked a thought further, she might have screamed; if she had beheld and comprehended all its pinnacles and caverns, she must certainly have swooned. The eccentric little that she saw affected her with a moderate pang of pity; her intuition was limited, but fair and lenient. It would be a cruel wrong to Clara to believe that rumour which at a later date identified her with the Lady Clara Vere de Vere of Mr. Tennyson's celebrated verses.

Mr. Hazard, on the other hand, saw a number of things which were not truly there, or perhaps it were juster to say that he perceived behind the shapes of actuality a multitude of informing spirits. The exact section of his mind into which Clara's neat pocket insight penetrated was the part wherewith he looked at Clara and the two girls and observed every charming detail of their forms and countenances, their lips and eyes and the ruffled locks of their hair making a magical spectrum of colour in the sun. Clara was pale chestnut and rose-ivory and amethystine-blue; Rosa was auburn

and pink-coral and hazel-grey; Allegra was flax
and snow and aquamarine. Mr. Hazard had never
taken an interest in muslin frocks; the nymphs of
his imagination were clothed in their own brightness, or in a cloud, or in the shadowy abun-
dance of their tresses. The cashmeres and merinos,
the grosgrain silks and Lyons velvet of his wife's
wardrobe had made a sober rainbow of black and
violet and crimson, but their rich fabric had
evoked no mystery. Now he was bewitched by the
fancy that the muslin frocks of Clara and her girls
had been accurately matched to the several colours of their eyes. These greys and azures were at
home among the willow-trees, between heaven
and the curve of heaven reflected in the stream.
The girls' thin skirts, which were so short as to
leave their fragile ankles free, were spattered with
river water; there was an engaging plumy disorder
in their curls. Even Clara, the veritable looking-
glass of grace and freshness, wore along the bor-
der of her blue gown a frosty pattern of dandelion
feathers; a few of these winged seeds clung like
snow-flakes to her soft brown hair.

From the swordblade edge of that sharp instant whereon his destiny had trembled, from the divided second of Clara's mercy or unkindness, Mr. Hazard's gratitude had sprung to meet her. His sick apprehension fell away from his heart; his pride was inviolate, she had not laid even the lightest finger-tip upon it. Yet she had known him, and known all about him; that lying all, that worse than nothing, that painstaking compilation of dead and rotting facts which his enemies would have called the truth. His pride scorned his enemies, and pitied them; it cared not a maggoty fig for their opinions. He cared for the opinions of very few; his friends need never be afraid of sitting down thirteen to table. Seven was a lucky number, and so, at the mouth of the pit, was three. Certainly he could count on three. But here, standing before him in a nimbus of sunset, were three more whom he desired as friends; by some incredible wizardry of fortune they did not turn away their faces from his wish.

Clara saw enough of his mind to be amused and flattered; had she seen even half of it, she would have fled from bother and responsibility like an elusive doe. She had a sensible faith in her own skill in dealing with black sheep of respectable family, and she knew there were no dove-cots to be fluttered within the confines of her garden. Her girls were darting swallows, who would chatter and laugh at wolves and poor black sheep alike.

In the far valleys and upon the mountain-tops of Mr. Hazard's mind walked shapes invisible to Clara. Each of the three figures standing before him in haloes of sunset had a brighter double upon the mountain-tops. These spirits stepped barefoot over the snows; they descended into the valleys to bathe in lucid streams. They were his sisters, and at the same time they were Clara and Rosa and Allegra. They were his children, and at the same time they were Rosa and Allegra.

It must be admitted that Lionel was not among this silver company. He was at San Sebastian with his adoring mother, quite safe, quite stout and healthy, quite satisfied with his worthy and important self. He was now nearly fourteen years old, and his firm little mind had already decided that he did not like his father. Lionel felt that this was a pity; he would never have expected to love Mr. Hazard, but he believed that with a few real efforts towards improvement upon his father's part it might have been possible to like him within reason. Mr. Hazard did not make these efforts. He seemed to consider it the whole duty of parents to be kind and devoted, to impart knowledge with brilliant patience, to listen indulgently to all one had to say, to take one for long lonely walks and to teach one to sail a fishing-smack. Mr. Hazard's theory of pleasures and accomplishments might have been evolved upon another planet than Lionel's. He never even tried to dress like other people's fathers, or to go to church, or to procure a pony or a tutor for Lionel. Lionel could not help disapproving of his father; he was far too virtuous to think this a correct filial sentiment, but he could not help it. Privately Lionel thought Mr. Hazard a thoroughly detrimental father.

Lionel's thoughts were not so private as his complacency supposed; Mr. Hazard was well aware of his son's sentiments. He was sincerely fond of Lionel, but he thought him a prig. Mr. Hazard felt that this was a pity. When Lionel regarded him with cold and ill-concealed disapprobation, Mr. Hazard forced himself to smile.

When he was alone, he forced himself to laugh; nevertheless he suffered a profound mortification in the knowledge that Lionel did not like him. Lionel strongly resembled his distinguished grandfather Mr. Baddeley, and Mr. Baddeley detested Mr. Hazard. Mr. Hazard had grown used to the situation; he never worried his wife by referring to it. But he did not consider it necessary to allow Lionel to roam at will among the far valleys and upon the mountain-tops of his secret mind. The lost company of children was innocent of Lionel's presence; Lionel would have disapproved of them all.

Clara watched Mr. Hazard; the cloud of these reflections sent shadows of reverie across his face. Its lines were deepened or erased as he contemplated a sorrow or an absurdity. He had not spoken for at least three minutes.

"Ridiculous creature!" Clara thought tolerantly, "But I suppose he's had rather a hard time of it. He can't have found all those odd dreary people particularly to his taste. He isn't vain or bad-tempered, like Alonzo Raven; he's bewildered. 'Blank misgivings . . .' as someone says.

It's not to be wondered at that he finds us an agreeable change after *that* galley. I believe I shall ask him to dinner one day; it's evident that he's never had enough to eat since his family disowned him!"

7

Drowned Lyonnesse

SIR JOHN HUNTING was in Persia; therefore he could not possibly forbid his wife to ask Mr. Hazard to dinner one day. It is to be presumed that he had his own reasons for going to Persia; certainly they were nobody else's reasons, for Sir John took nobody into his confidence. It appeared to be his stubborn determination to beat Colonel Passmore's detachment by at least six months; since he went alone, the East India Company was contemptuously silent. As Lord Camphile's son-in-law he had been a privileged person; his vagaries were licensed during Gerald's lifetime. But Gerald had been dead these three years, and now the directors had received a letter from Lord William Bentinck begging them not to allow Sir John to come to India again. The Governor-General wrote pathetically of nervous dyspepsia and the strain upon his good manners, and the board was happy to assure him that Sir John Hunting was by now exploring Susiana or Elymais, instructing a regiment of Azerbaijan infantry, or composing a memoir on the Atropatenian Ecbatana for the *Journal of the Royal Geographical Society*. As a matter of fact, he was attempting to decipher the cuneiform inscriptions on the rock tablets of Behistun; his discoveries antedated those of Major Rawlinson, but were not crowned with the same wreath of public honours.

Clara deplored his absence with dutiful regret, but she was too happily her mother's daughter to regard an erratic husband as a question of prime importance. Hers was a riddle rather than a question, but her desire to solve the riddle had languished into mild incurious content. She was interested in her children, who adored her. Clara was an enchanting mother; she teased and scolded them in dazzling turn. Her loving mockery was excellent discipline; she could be tender, and although she could be stern, she always forgave them by bedtime.

She felt a slight maternal interest in the unfortunate Mr. Hazard; she was younger than he, but she believed that she was infinitely wiser. She dispatched a pretty little note to his lodgings, inviting him to dine at Lyonnesse upon the following Friday evening.

"Lyonnesse? Can it really be called Lyonnesse?" thought Mr. Hazard as he read the note on a rainy afternoon, with the skies falling upon his smoking fire in sooty black drops. There was the name in gilt letters at the top of the cream-coloured note-paper, yet it seemed too good to be true. His memory of Clara and her girls was fading, as a rainbow fades among wet grey clouds. Allegra was the sea-blue fringe of a rainbow dissolving in the storm.

Mr. Hazard had returned several times to the green door through which he used to emerge into an earlier spring, but although he could see his former self quite plainly, a flushed and breathless stripling in a long brown coat with curling lamb's-wool collar and cuffs, he never caught, even from the corner of his eye, the briefest flicker of light from those younger ghosts whom he hunted along West Street. People emerged; senseless memories emerged at intervals, and then in the hush of waiting his heart would skip a beat, and he would be visited by a premonition of horror. So he would turn and stride back to his lodgings, and if he were not too brutally shaken by the blind encounter, he would apply himself with vehement diligence to the Book of Job, making of his verse a double bridle to bind leviathan.

At the end of five days his mind misgave him; he must be watching the wrong covert. He took various long walks, carrying *Paradise Lost* in one pocket and a hunch of bread and cheese in the other. The woods were freaked and pied with fresh transparent leaves and flowers; the sound of the birds fell with the sunlight, dizzily sweet from above. Nowhere between the forest-trees did he perceive his quarry. The conviction lay cold upon his spirit that only in the slender crystal facets of Allegra's face could he perceive it; perhaps he would never see Allegra again.

Therefore Clara's note came to him as a white dove out of the stormy afternoon; its olive-branch shone like a cluster of pearls. He had walked over to Windsor Great Park that morning; it was shrouded in unrevealing mist, and he had returned to Gravelow through a driving rain. Now he could not work, or even stop the fire from smoking. He was on the bleak point of deciding to go back to Spain when the lodging-house servant brought him Clara's note. It made pleasanter reading than young Mr. Bulwer's novel, *Eugene Aram*, which Annamaria had given him as a parting gift. It had been an error to suppose that *Eugene Aram* was light reading suitable to a rainy day; Clara had provided the only reading possible in such weather.

Friday was fine; the leaves glittered after the rain like the plumage of a million peacocks. Mr. Hazard was waked at four o'clock by a jagged rejoicing sound of cock-crow; his heart gave a leap and he was broad awake in an instant. He laughed to think that he had seized the earliest moments of this day because he desired it, because he could not lie submissively asleep after its bright edge had dipped itself in sunlight. The impatient hammering of his heart drummed him out of bed and into the garden; he walked up and down the garden in his dressing-gown, marvelling at the drops of dew as if each had been a special miracle.

When the clear amber of morning had turned into the cloudy amber of afternoon, Mr. Hazard dressed himself with extreme care; his elegance was slightly formal and old-fashioned, but it became him the better for this singularity. It never occurred to him to hire a chaise from the inn; he considered the skiff, but in the end he set off on foot.

The rain had laid the dust; it was not unreasonable to go on foot through such an afternoon. A faint mist melted the morning's colours to opalescence, and blanched the sun to the moon's paler gold. Mr. Hazard climbed the winding paths of the Quarry Wood and went down into the valley. The hedgerows were like green waves whose crests of foam had been magically stayed at the moment of breaking. Mr. Hazard plucked the hawthorn and sniffed its bitter fragrance as he went.

Presently he saw a lane that ran between high walls, and at the corner of the lane a painted sign, with the word *Lyonnesse* written upon it. The lane was longer than he had supposed, and it had many turnings; now it ran under trees, and now between meadows where taller trees lifted their latticed branches against the cloudy hem of the west.

At last he saw the house clear at the end of a vista, and then it disappeared, and he saw it again under an archway of trees. It had been built less than forty years ago, of yellow brick and stone; he had seen it often, in sharp relief against the air and in wavering reflection in the stream, as he passed in his boat along the river. He remembered it very well now; it was a strange house, and he had always been charmed by its forward-thrusting shape above the water. It hung there like a castle or a crag; the severity of its outline was touched with Gothic fantasy.

From the river it was a promontory, but now its tawny fabric made it into a golden tower in the sun. Its lawns were striped and chequered with light, so that half lay like a field of gilt damask and half like a tapestry of blue and violet shade. There was a copper beech upon the lawn, and its thin new leaves were not metal, but flame.

Clara was waiting for Mr. Hazard upon the stone terrace; she did not appear in the least surprised to see him come on foot. She wore a frock of crisp white muslin, with wide diaphanous sleeves gathered into bands about her wrists like the sleeves of some pastoral bishop in a fairy-tale. There was a blue sash tied at her waist and a transparent blue kerchief knotted below her throat. She looked as fresh as if she had fallen from the rain-washed sky and were still wound in its tinted veils.

Mr. Hazard was somewhat tired, because he had been awake since four o'clock that morning; the sight of Clara was grateful to his senses as a glass of iced wine. He was aware that his shoes were dusty, and that Clara's hand was cool and fragile as she touched his hand.

"I am glad to see you," said Clara in her sweet voice, which held more intricate stops and modulations than most people's voices. "How nice that you could come to us today and what luck to have such perfect weather! Here are the girls coming up from the river; you will have to be properly introduced this time."

Mr. Hazard turned towards the river; he saw Rosa running up the path in a pink frock. Allegra followed three steps behind her, but Mr. Hazard could not see the colour of Allegra's frock. The delicate irregular radiance of Allegra's face was a clear crystal wherein Mr. Hazard beheld the pure and absolute image of beauty, clothed in its own brightness and borne along by the wind of its own speed. The crystal of Allegra's face was a clear chalice, filled with immaculate beauty to the brim.

8

Unlacing of a Breastplate

"SHALL we have tea in the saloon, or tell them to bring it out to the terrace?" asked Clara after dinner, certain that nobody but a blind man would choose the saloon with the prospect of sunset and moonrise before him. She knew that Mr. Hazard was not blind; his large disquieting eyes had rested longer upon her face than upon the laughing faces of her children, and already she had seen that Allegra's grace had tranced and enchanted his mind. He looked at Clara with his eyes and at Allegra with the inner vision of his mind. Clara was not disturbed by this trick of double perception upon the part of Mr. Hazard; she told herself that she was the only person present who was not a child or a bewildered dreamer more easily led than any child. She felt herself capable of leading Mr. Hazard away from his vision should occasion ever demand this measure, and she suspected that although he loved Allegra, the girl was no more to him than an alabaster shell filled with the light of his own spirit. If Mr. Hazard wished to find a friend among them, he must choose Clara.

Mr. Hazard had already chosen her; already she was invested in the splendour of his imagination. Whatever might have been one's opinion of Mr. Hazard in his twentieth year, at forty he looked invulnerable and coldly withdrawn. This frigid demeanour was a deliberately contrived effect; this was his armour. It was heavy and crossgrained upon his heart; he looked at Clara and he saw a friend, and little by little the joints of his armour were loosened. It fell away from his breast; it was as though the weight of a millstone had fallen. He laid aside the heaviness of years, and drew his breath lightly and without pain. His sharp sigh of relief drew kindness from the air; he was tired, and he wondered how he had ever borne that load of cruel steel over his heart.

"On the terrace, don't you think, in honour of the moon?" asked Clara with her most accomplished smile. Mr. Hazard thought with Clara, but if she had suggested the boot-hole he would have followed her choice contentedly. In showering Clara with the attributes of divinity Mr. Hazard denied her the power to do evil, even in lesser things. If she had bidden him drink the essential oil of bitter almonds instead of China tea, Mr. Hazard would have drained the venomous cup. He had not trusted a living soul for seven interminable years, and now it was a fire-new delight to trust Clara.

Mr. Hazard and Clara walked slowly up and down upon the terrace while the two girls ran races upon the lawn below. "Outrageous little hoydens," said Clara, knowing well that they were prettier than painted moths in the twilight. Presently she sat down in a great chair that was curved and silvered like a sea-shell. "They were made for the grotto, and then the grotto was too damp," said Clara, but Mr. Hazard felt that they had been made for Clara.

He sat upon the stone balustrade of the

terrace; he would have been more comfortable in one of the scalloped arm-chairs, but Mr. Hazard had never cared to be comfortable when he was happy. Perhaps the two states of being might not flourish together in his heart, and he had wearied of striving to reconcile them. He was very happy; he marvelled at his seven years of bitter and suspicious pride. He thought contemptuously of pride; it was not courage, it was after all a recreant and ignoble thing to go armed and armoured and panoplied in that precaution. He looked at Clara and Clara looked at him. The risen moon and the sun inclining towards the west mingled rose and silver-gold in the serene air; these beams were conformable to Clara's face, but not to Mr. Hazard's whose severely carven features shed their flattering dyes as a swimmer's forehead sheds the water.

"Amethystine," thought Mr. Hazard.

"Absurd creature," thought Clara, "I wish he did not look so ill, but perhaps it is only because he is wearing such a very odd cravat."

They talked of the children, and then because the children's antics wove a Grecian frieze upon Mr. Hazard's fancy, they talked of Athens, and from Athens their talk shifted by way of Sparta and Thermopylæ to Persian affairs, and soon they were talking of the East India Company and the late Lord Camphile, and Mr. Hazard was telling how he had once begged Mr. Bird to procure him employment at the court of an Indian prince, in some secret and political capacity. He had been sorry to learn that such employment was open only to regular servants of the Company.

"But I could not see why I should not be a regular servant," said Mr. Hazard with a slight smile, and Clara laughed and told him that he had not the air of a regular servant of anything so incorporated as a company.

"Of Prospero, perhaps," said Clara, being kind, and remembering the trapped and shining prisoner of the Venetian tea-party. Mr. Hazard's short laugh was merciless to himself; he thought of Caliban, but he did not care, because he was happy.

"'Have a new master, get a new man!'" thought Mr. Hazard.

9

Private View of the Invisible

MR. HAZARD walked home by moonlight; the dust seemed impalpable as air beneath his tread. He had forgotten all that austere and patient schooling with which he had sought to inform his mind during the last difficult years, or else his temerity was mocking its lessons in a mood of reckless elation. He had drunk several cups of green tea, but its pale infusion was not sufficient cause for the powerful impulse of joy which bore him onward along an airy path of moonlight. His everyday tastes would have bidden him listen for a nightingale under the flying arches of the wood, but tonight he did not bother about nightingales. The singing of the blood in his ears was set to a light vivacious measure, and he would have been sorry to have its sacred levity darkened by the voice of a bewailing nightingale.

"It will keep you awake, you know; you won't sleep a wink if you take another cup," Clara had told him maternally as she gave him the tea. She would have preferred to give him Turkish coffee, which she made in a pretty contrivance which her father had brought her from Constantinople. Clara loved to make the coffee; it was such a pleasant game that she was sure the sweet resulting syrup could keep nobody awake.

"Nothing ever keeps me awake," said Mr. Hazard mendaciously. He disliked Turkish coffee, because it resembled the muddy brew he had been reduced to drinking in the cave of the chief Odysseus. He had no wish to sleep or to dream while the true world contained Allegra and Clara.

Even as he left them and walked away from the Gothic tower of Lyonnesse, he was well content with the world and with his own share in its revolving fortunes. He compared his present condition to the worser states of the influenza and thought himself luckily recovered. All things were comparative; a boy of twenty hastening to his first assignation might believe this thin gentleman who walked so lightly upon dust to be broken and worn and middle-aged, but Mr. Hazard understood the liberal value of solitude, and he was glad to be alone and with his face turned from Lyonnesse. He had no more desire to steal its enchanting creatures for mortal employ than to fling a noose round the moon and pull it earthward to be cherished in his breast.

Nevertheless he was aware of his happy chance in having found a friend like Clara. She was the fine essence, the seventh distillation of his milder, more Platonic loves, those charming, melancholy loves which had been so much less exhausting than the passions. Yes, Clara was of that graceful number, but above them in her exquisite calm and distinction; she was as the evening-star to a wreath of bright tapers. She might never be willing to read Plutarch before breakfast or to play the guitar after tea, but she would be sure to turn such hours to uses of her own, to fill them with the casual poetry of her gestures and the musical concord of her voice. She was mistress of more influential harmonies than may be evoked from the strings of a guitar.

As to his few excessive passions, their memory pricked his nerves to a joyless agitation, and he did well to forget them if he was to endure the common stress of business with ease and self-command. Whether the business of his life was to be fomenting revolution or composing heroic verse, he did well to eschew the memory of those fevers. His Platonic loves were another matter; a cool, allaying recollection, temperate as Athenian marble.

It is not the province of this chronicle to pronounce a moral or intellectual judgment upon Mr. Hazard's virtues and defects. In the opinion of many persons of good sense and eminent faculties he had been a wiser and a more admirable man had he now proceeded to fall in love with his landlady's daughter or to take the barmaid of the Crown to his actual heart. Others would have advised him to make immediate haste to Portsmouth and to embark without delay upon a vessel bound for Spanish ports. Neither of these meritorious courses occurred to Mr. Hazard. He believed it a mistake to fall in love with one's inferiors; the ardent spirit of his youth had betrayed him into this error more than once, and the ensuing shocks had rendered him incapable of its repetition, and undesirous of the bad essay. The Spanish voyage was inevitable, but his conscience had set it for September, and it had not the barbarity to goad him to dutiful change of plan as he strode along the moonlit path to Gravelow. It would have been a harsh inflictive conscience that had harassed Mr. Hazard as he walked alone in the regenerated quiet of his soul.

For the first time in seven years he seemed to possess his soul in patience. Now for the moment he regretted nothing, he demanded nothing even of his own driven and conscripted powers. Beyond the light clear fabric of his thoughts, beyond the tranquillity of his thoughts unravelled from their horrid knots and smoothly braided into order, he perceived Allegra. Clara had untied the knots and soothed the tangles of his mind; she had accomplished this miracle without effort, by the subtle expedient of her smiles. But Allegra could do far more than this; the sharp irregular facets of her little face provided a glass for divination and subliminal wisdom. This emotion was not Platonic, or romantic, or animal; it was not love, but revelation.

To determine Mr. Hazard a madman and a fool would be precipitate and inept to the point of folly. It is enough to admit that he was mistaken. The emotion that he now experienced was love; Mr. Hazard was too proud, too scrupulous and too sensitive to recognize the recurrent spell. He had not been in love for five adventurous years, save for a brief passion of pity for a prostitute at Salonika, and he no longer believed himself to be a fit vessel for that holy element. He had never been vain, and certain private crosses had convinced him that he was too detached and bitter, too irritable, and, above all, too indifferent to inspire devotion in a fellow mortal. When he thought of Caliban, his thought was not ironical; Mr. Hazard would have made a preposterously refined monster, but his grotesque fancy was quite sincere. Moreover, he believed that he was so far insensible and disillusioned as to be sadly guarded against the assaults of love.

He was not, perhaps, unaware that in the past he had often filled a hollow alabaster shell with the light of his own spirit, but in the past his spirit had been volatile and brilliant, and evident as a burning planet within the trivial lantern where he had been pleased to kindle it. Now he did not recognize the darker star of his spirit within the image of Allegra, and if he had recognized it he would have been overcome by an impersonal anger against himself. He would have thought himself profoundly unfitted to feel a true and pitiful human love for Allegra; by force of scrupulous horror he would have murdered the sentiment in his own bosom. But Mr. Hazard did not suspect the pathetic fact; he was upheld by an implicit belief that the emotion which now possessed and pierced his heart was not love, but revelation.

He raised his eyes to the lineaments of heaven, and beheld the broad circle of stars dissolved in moonlight, drowning in the flood of thin radiance emanated from the moon. The eternal stars were small and perished flames in that vast, cold, pervasive flood of moonlight.

Mr. Hazard was happy, and so it never occurred to him to be afraid of the moon. He walked until the dawn came up with music from the east. The dawn, in Mr. Hazard's eyes as he turned homeward, seemed stained with the rose of predestined joy and plainly elected to a secret calendar of festivals. It is true that Mr. Hazard's odd theories concerning sunrise were untenable, but he had been awake for precisely twenty-four hours and had walked a mile for every hour of his waking.

10

Butter and Honey

Now, as the rainbow wave of spring arose and broke and flung a glittering spray of flowers into the air and then subsided into the long, smooth swell of summer, there began for Mr. Hazard a little silver age, so peaceable and hushed that it seemed secure against the hurry and violence of an ending. It was an age no longer golden, but it seemed the safer for that moderation; it was so small, so quiet, and so sweetly hedged about that it appeared exempt from envy and evil fortune. It was a paradise of children, but for Mr. Hazard, who was forty years old, it was no more than a middle land, a merciful limbo swept by tempered airs and calm with the lowered sun of twilight. After the ambiguous battles and the loud confusion of the past it was far better than happiness.

Clara was very kind to him. She soon learned him by heart, and Clara's heart, though cool and thrifty, was quick to learn the symbols and curious traits which traced the outward character of Mr. Hazard. To her it was as simple as a nonsense alphabet, or a blind man's language to be deciphered by her clever finger-tips. Nevertheless, she liked Mr. Hazard; otherwise she would never have allowed him to come to Lyonnesse once or twice every week during May and June.

"He isn't a villain, and he isn't exactly a lunatic," she told her friends, who wondered how Clara could possibly put up with Mr. Hazard. "He is simply an absurd creature, an odd fish very much out of water among the Cockney illuminati, a black sheep unconsciously homesick for the fold. His talents are considerable, I assure you; you know that I have scant patience with poetry, but I believe his reputation is advancing by leaps and bounds and somersaults into places where even you may meet it. Him you will never meet; he wouldn't be a bit more tolerant of you than you are of him, dearest Edwina."

Edwina, or Matilda, or Amelia, as the case might be, would look delicately incredulous at this statement, but it was no stranger than the truth. The lady would no more hurriedly have let down her blonde lace veil and departed in her barouche than Mr. Hazard would have dropped his book, stooped to pick it up again, and fled to the point or the plantation. Clara had no trouble with cuts and *contretemps;* if the world regarded Mr. Hazard as defiling pitch, Mr. Hazard was at extreme pains to keep himself unspotted from the world. Clara was the best of good friends with both, for Clara belonged to the gay and self-sufficient world, and Mr. Hazard, in these hypnotic hours, belonged to Clara.

She liked him well enough to be carelessly flattered by his devotion; she thought his judgment sound in selecting her as a type of titulary saint, while he avoided the company of her acquaintances as though they had been so many elegant ghouls and succubi. It was a nice discriminating distinction, which stroked the pigeon feathers of Clara's gentle vanity until they shone like the outer skin of a pearl. The dreaming docility of Mr. Hazard's manner towards Clara was in piquant contrast to his wild runaway recoil from her country neighbours. In his more philosophic moods he would even submit to holding the Berlin wool for her embroidery, but if an inoffensive female in a fashionable bonnet approached with the tiniest rustle of silks, he turned chalky white and disappeared.

He was extraordinarily biddable, and his persistent innocence was a continual outrage to Clara's polished common sense. Nevertheless, it was a convenient quality; a dexterous touch might mould it, like clean wax, to any fabulous shape or pattern. It was a source of vexed amusement to Clara to observe how deeply her idlest word could impress the pure and malleable substance of Mr. Hazard's innocence.

"Let me see, how old will your Lionel be next November?" Clara would inquire sweetly. "Ah, fourteen; perhaps he's a trifle young for Allegra, but what fun if they should fancy each other! She's very much of a child at sixteen, isn't she?"

"Completely a child," Mr. Hazard would reply, his eyes upon Allegra's shining head as it dipped and skimmed in the distance. "It is a pity that she must ever grow up. But I should account myself the most fortunate of fathers to make such a water-nymph my daughter, if such dreams need not always go by contraries."

"He doesn't know I'm teasing him," thought Clara, suppressing both her mirth and her impatience. "He's impossible to snub, because he insists upon taking one's most frivolous remarks at their solemn face value. I meant to remind him that he's old enough to be Allegra's father, and to hint that it's ridiculous to adore her as he does, and instead I've only sent him into a happy reverie about settlements and silver-mounted corals."

Clara's verbal skill and Mr. Hazard's thin-skinned and fastidious taste were united in an effort to invalidate the fact of Mr. Hazard's tragic and unequal love. Between them they succeeded in an occult subversion of the truth which had the doubtful merit of deceiving them both. Clara began to remind herself that Lionel, in spite of his father's heterodox opinions, was the heir to solid advantages, and Mr. Hazard was so certain that his passion for Allegra was transcendentally paternal that any opposing arguments would have sickened him into memories of Saturn's reign.

"You must be kind to him, children; the poor

creature loves you to distraction," Clara told her girls in discreet plural. It was evident to anyone with wide bright eyes in her head that Allegra was Mr. Hazard's favourite, yet Rosa was kinder to him than Allegra ever stopped to be. Rosa was just and compassionate; she never lost her temper with Mr. Hazard as Allegra occasionally did, and she even had the patience to lie in a punt and listen to the lesser choruses of *Job: A Lyrical Drama.*

"Appropriate!" said Allegra. "How can you possibly help laughing when he comes to the part about the island of the innocent and the pureness of hands? He *is* so fond of that bit! You are an angel, and I hope he's sufficiently grateful."

"I don't mind it very much," said Rosa charitably. "In fact, I'm not at all sure that I don't rather enjoy it, on a hot afternoon. '*Job: A Lyrical Lullaby*'; it's a nice sleepy sound, like far-away thunder."

Occasionally Mr. Hazard would write little verses upon the leaves of his note-book, and tear them out, and give them to Clara or Rosa. He never gave them to Allegra, because he knew that Allegra did not like verses. Perhaps Mr. Hazard had guessed this dislike, or perhaps Allegra had told him when she lost her temper. Neither Clara nor Rosa shared her prejudice; Mr. Hazard's verses were very short and very narrow, a light sprinkling of words down the middle of a torn page. "Lovely," Rosa would say with a smile, and Clara would say: "Charming," or "How pretty," and mean it.

Mr. Hazard was content with this middle state; he found it better than happiness. He moved in an elegiac atmosphere; he was secluded and absolved from all extremities of the heart, and his mind had forbidden himself to grieve or to provoke him by questions or commands. The populated waste of London, the withering storms and icy strictures of his fever, the quicksands and the broken bridges of the further past, these things receded and were whirled away from him, until they appeared no larger than a cone-shaped cloud, a pillar of sharp particles of dust. The present closed upon him like a hermit's cell, clear and symmetrical, and full of sunlight as a bee's cell is full of honey.

II

Plenty of Cream with the Strawberries

THAT year's strawberry crop was uncommonly fine, which was fortunate, because Mr. Hazard was so very fond of strawberries that he had almost enough to eat so long as they were in season. Certainly they were an incomparable fruit for anyone who preferred not to lift his eyes from the pages of a book, even while he was dining. Cherries had stones, and gooseberries had hairy skins; an apple must be peeled and quartered, and that was an undertaking that stole his hands and eyes away from the Hebrew Testament. The dates of Arabia were both stony and sticky, and Seville oranges required one's entire mind. Peaches and grapes were almost worth the bother, but the bother was there, between him and the book; a melon was nearly as bad as a knock on the door. There was nothing in the world like a strawberry, cleanly moulded as a flower, and with its frilled stem providing a neat handle which even the most absent-minded person must appreciate. While there were strawberries to be had in the markets of Gravelow, there was no real danger that Mr. Hazard would starve.

For the sake of Job, and the virgin surface of his foolscap, Mr. Hazard ate his strawberries without sugar or cream when he dined alone in his lodgings. What else he ate is a matter for pure conjecture, not to be determined by an examination of Mr. Hazard's weekly bills. Fowls were bought; cutlets in immoderate quantities; ducks upon occasion, and profuse green peas and carrots. These were pleasant days for Mr. Hazard's landlady, but such is the rank ingratitude of human nature that by the end of June she resented Mr. Hazard's inroads upon his own brown loaf and Cheddar cheese, and stared indignantly at the empty dish when he was hungry enough to eat all his own strawberries.

Mr. Hazard had succeeded in reconciling Job and John Milton's Satan to a perfect concord; the other Satan, the Satan of the Hebrew Testament, was busy going to and fro in the earth, and walking up and down in it, while he devised elaborate torments for Job. This Satan was not a sympathetic character, yet sometimes Mr. Hazard liked him better than Job. He remained in the company of these from nine o'clock in the morning until the table was laid for dinner, but in the evening he escaped to John Milton's Satan. He wandered for miles up and down the valley of the Thames, sometimes in the skiff and sometimes on foot, and perhaps once a week Clara sent him a little gilt-edged note inviting him to Lyonnesse.

When he dined with Clara, he had plenty of cream with his strawberries; Clara saw to that, for she had a shrewd and amused suspicion that he lived upon watercress and monastic lentils when he was out of her sight. By intuitive enchantments untouched by vulgar curiosity Clara had discovered quite as much about the influenza and the broken ribs and the pistol ball as Mr. Hazard could remember, and possibly a little bit more. She was aware of Mr. Hazard's genius for making himself uncomfortable, and vaguely, carelessly aware of another and far different sort of genius, lighting its intermittent fires within the ravaged framework of his body. Partly in true charity of heart and partly in childlike vanity Clara took pains to make Mr. Hazard more comfortable than he had ever been since his family disowned him; she was very proud of the gentle wonders she accomplished without effort or particular thought. It was white magic, the more remarkable because she never exercised it above once or at most twice a week. It was pleasant to ameliorate the sad state of Mr. Hazard's nerves and to make the holes under his cheek-bones less conspicuous, but at the same time Clara felt that it would never do to spoil him. Once a week was enough; twice was a feast of indulgence.

It is an affecting commentary upon Mr. Hazard's way of life that such an amelioration should have been wrought in his comfort by Clara's casual kindness. He was quite capable of taking care of himself had he chosen to do so, but he did not choose; it never occurred to him to take care of himself. The project was too dull for his imagination; in a storm or a battle or a revolutionary plan he was eminently cool and courageous, but in lodgings in Gravelow he was not tempted to take thought to save his skin. In Mr. Hazard's sardonic opinion his skin was not worth saving. As to conserving his energies and guarding his powers, he had wasted and spent these things in a thousand vain endeavours, but at least he had flung them upon the hurricane, and scattered them upon the face of the sea. They were not worn away in fear and safety and avarice of the spirit.

Nevertheless his wild prodigality had been hard upon Mr. Hazard; the past ten years had exhausted him. Clara knew the limits of his strength better than he cared to know them; she saw that he had come to the thin frayed end of his tether, the strained and tightened thread. Softly and insensibly she drew him back through a labyrinth of weariness; he would never have retraced its arid paths alone. Her hand was light and fragile as it rested upon his, and with the utmost ease she drew him back to life.

She gave him plenty of cream with his strawberries, and she did not laugh when he looked at Allegra. Clara did not believe in spoiling Mr. Hazard, but perhaps she spoiled him a little, against her colder judgment. She felt very sorry for him when he looked at Allegra, and so she poured more cream upon his strawberries, and did not even smile.

"He works too hard at that ridiculous poem," thought Clara. "And of course he does not eat enough, or go to bed at a reasonable hour. It's entirely his own fault; I have no patience with such folly. But I wish he did not look so ill."

"We are going for a picnic next Wednesday afternoon," said Clara weakly. "Do come with us, if it would amuse you. When the boys come home for the holidays, we must have plenty of picnics."

12

Sheer o'er the Chrystal Battlements

THE Monday before the picnic brought Mr. Hazard a long letter from Annamaria; he read it impatiently, crumpling its closely written sheets in irritable fingers. Her crossed and interlined pages closed upon his brain like a net upon a flying creature; the Hexateuch was less wearying to his eyes. By the time he had deciphered the letter he had a headache, and his conscience, which was even more sensitive than his optic nerve, was painfully affected.

"My dear Hazard," wrote Annamaria in vivid violet ink, "we are convinced that you are lonely.

Coulson says he saw you in Maidenhead last week and that he could not in common honesty give us a good account of your looks. We are considering a little holiday in Dorset at Lulworth Cove or some such pretty spot and should be very happy for your company. The Carlyles have asked us to Craigenputtock, but naturally we cannot afford the journey. What would you say if we turned up at Gravelow one of these fine mornings and took lodgings next door to you? I am sure we should cheer you up amazingly in your 'retired leisure' and I would make it my particular care to tyrannize over you in the matter of flannel waistcoats and cod-liver oil."

Mr. Hazard leaned back against the broken springs of the sofa and closed his eyes; the letter fell to the floor, crushed into a crackling ball of paper. "Good God; cod-liver oil!" said Mr. Hazard in a whisper which rustled less audibly than the crushed pages of the letter.

He knew, of course, that he must ask the Hartleighs to visit him. His imagination conjured up a score of dutiful reasons, presented to his pity like so many waxwork groups wherein the Hartleighs' domestic misfortunes were modelled in crude emotional blood and tears. The forced and vulgar gaiety of Annamaria's letter was infinitely pathetic and infinitely repulsive to his mind. He would willingly have paid a thousand pounds by means of ruinous post-obits to be spared the necessity of writing the affectionate note which invited his friends to join him at Gravelow without delay.

"They are certain to come Wednesday," he told himself shortly; he had nothing but contempt for the cold inhospitable distaste at the core of his heart. But on Wednesday there was a letter by the first post explaining that someone had lent the Hartleighs a cottage at Hythe. "A rose-bowered cot," Annamaria called it. "There will always be a bed for you, Hazard, and a welcome kept warm upon the hob."

"Excellent creature," said Mr. Hazard, with an acid smile for his happy deliverance; he had an honest scorn for his own squeamishness. He perceived quite plainly that Annamaria was possessed of sterling virtues which Clara's elegant mockery had thinned to gilded filigree; nevertheless he preferred Clara's cooler welcome, and the lighter clasp of her more delicate hand.

Clara's welcome was cool as the slim bottle of hock, sealed with mauve wax and necklaced with a princely coat of arms, which lay half hidden in green water under the willow trees. The day was very hot; the sun absorbed the colour of the sky, which fainted through gradations of blue and crystal to transparency.

"I knew you would be tired," said Clara with a sidelong glance at Mr. Hazard; his boots and his black trousers were trimmed with a disreputable ermine of dust. "You look a little like one of those unlucky magic images which some enemy has melted away to nothingness in front of a raging fire. Why on earth didn't you come by the river on such a morning? We meant to make you row us to a more romantic solitude, but now we shall have to give you a very cold luncheon before you will be fit for it."

"I am not tired," said Mr. Hazard somewhat stiffly, "and I think this is a deplorably dull place for a picnic. I had far rather row you to Taplow or Bisham; it is too early for luncheon."

"Now you are cross," said Clara, laughing, "I knew that you were tired; you are never cross or rude except when you are tired. We are all of us starving, but I suppose we shall have to wait until you have rowed us up stream for ever before you will allow us a leaf of lettuce or a drop of ginger-beer; it is very tiresome of you."

To herself she murmured: "Absurd creature!" and "Preposterous vanity!" while her kind heart accorded him several excuses for petulance. It must be excessively fatiguing to walk five miles under a broiling sun, with one's pockets full of heavy books, and one's thin flesh fretted by mortifying thorns of weariness. It must be galling to know that one's hair was grey instead of silver-gold or russet; it must be vexing to wear a damp shirt and dusty black trousers while lovelier beings were immaculate in linen lawn. Clara forgave Mr. Hazard for his captious pride; she took the honey of compliment from it and neatly removed its sting. Mr. Hazard's gratitude and relief were extreme; her smile went over him like a small wave, washing the dust from his brow.

"We will compromise," said Clara in her

teasing and caressing voice. "You shall row us as far as the weir, and we will make the greedy little girls eat drumsticks while you and I eat white meat, and we will drink a moderate quantity of Papa's Johannisberger out of brittle green glasses, and pour the rest into the river as a libation to Odin and a sacrifice to your principles. You will not appreciate it, but it will cure your headache. You may spare yourself the trouble of denying your headache, because at the end of half an hour it will be completely cured."

"How clever you are!" said Mr. Hazard as he fitted the oars into the rowlocks. "You make music without an instrument and compound medicines without a mortar and pestle. I never deny what you bid me believe; your advice is sibylline."

"You are very amiable to tell me so," said Clara, "and to give me pretty speeches in return for scolding you. Here are Rosa and Allegra longing to ask you whether you've remembered the songs; we hope you have the songs in your pocket and that you will read them to us before we've eaten the last strawberry. It will be delightful to have madrigals with our dessert."

"Yes," said Rosa, blushing with compassion, "we hope very much you've brought the songs; it was so nice of you to write them specially for us."

"Yes," said Allegra, "it was nice of you bothering to write us songs."

Mr. Hazard was not deceived; he knew that the light creature of his love was indifferent to madrigals. The severe brilliance of his inner mind sent its beam beyond the sparkling translucence of Allegra's spirit; she was clear to him body and soul. She would not have given a hollow green rush or a bright new pin for all the songs he had ever made. Nevertheless she was courteous and not unkind; there was no shadow of cruelty to mar her pure impersonal laughter. Her nonchalance could neither inflict a hurt nor heal it; she was innocent of the desire to wound and innocent of pity.

For no better reason that that he loved her, Mr. Hazard was satisfied. He felt that Allegra would have been spoiled by the most trivial improvement her flaws were more exquisite than perfections. He would never attempt to paint a snow-flake with the warmth and the rich odour of a rose.

"You think them pretty, don't you?" asked Clara with her gentlest mockery as she poured the yellow Rhine wine into the thin ice-coloured glasses. "No, I mean the little girls, not the engraved crystal."

After luncheon Mr. Hazard was tempted into reading his songs. The act was against his judgment and acquired wisdom, but Clara loosened the sinews of his will and he complied, aware of his own folly. He did not care; let him be ridiculous and have done with it, under the shade of the willows, to the Lethean murmur of the weir. The quiet, the cool scent of the river, the music of Clara's voice, the wine like chilled sunlight in the thin glass, the wind silvering the willow leaves, had driven away his headache and tempered his pulses to the smooth flow of the stream. His nerves were released from pain; the water clasping his wrist like a miraculous bracelet drew the fever from his blood. The boat was moored in shadow; a radiance, strained and filtered through nets of blue and green, fell upon Allegra's hair. All shapes were softened, all colours were diffused and dimmed. Even the cushions in the boat had faded to the purple-red of *pot-pourri*. Mr. Hazard had three of these cushions at his back; he drew his hand dripping from the river and found the songs in his pocket, as Clara bade him.

They were not really madrigals; they were small lyrics, in the simplest couplets and quatrains. Clara believed that Mr. Hazard had made the verses plain and simple to suit the understanding of children; she thought them charming and ingenuous.

"Mine is lovely," said Rosa, and Allegra said: "Mine is even nicer." They smiled, and wondered why Mr. Hazard's voice had grown hoarse upon the final syllables. He looked very tired, and more than ever like a scarecrow.

Mr. Hazard was tired, indeed, but singularly content. Clara had led him along a cool and level path of folly, and there was no punishment at the end of it, but only peace, and the children's thanks put into his hands like flowers. He regarded the wasted beauty of his songs as so many drops of honey wherewith to win the suffrages of butterflies.

"What fun we have had!" said Clara as he rowed them back to Lyonnesse on a river visibly dissolving in the rarer essence of evening light. "What a delicious afternoon! Next week the boys will be here; you must come again a week from today, and we will have another picnic, and you shall make friends with the boys and their tutor, Mr. Hodge. Good-bye, and don't forget to eat seven sensible dinners between now and next Wednesday."

The twilight was dissolving gold; Mr. Hazard was the one black mark upon the golden road to Gravelow. The day had drawn an unbroken circle of happiness round him, but now, as the day fell down for ever behind the curving edge of the earth, he shivered a little. He did not think of it as a prophetic shiver; there had been too many chills in the past, upon the slopes of Mount Parnassus and in the hollow vales of the Maremma, to put Mr. Hazard to the trouble of questioning the future about a little shiver along his spine.

Book Three

MR. HODGE

Book Three

MR. HODGE

I

A Deep Romantic Chasm

IF anyone ever takes the trouble nowadays to traverse the cloudy eminence of song which Mr. Hazard once builded upon the Book of Job, he may discover for himself that a certain peak of accomplishment outshines and overtops the rest. This is the third act; this is the lyric elevation which Mr. Hazard scaled during a week of June.

This week contained the longest day of the year, that revolving chariot whose wheels are thirteen circles of moonlight. The longest day, and the brief shadow of darkness cast by it, sufficed for the last chorus, which glittered like snow upon the summit of the rest.

Mr. Hazard was well pleased with his work; he paused and surveyed the earthier kingdoms below him and preferred the isolated tower he had made. He was at once the architect and the explorer of this place; the flying buttresses which supported it were his own powers, and he had cut steps out of cold heaven as he climbed. Now he was satisfied with the height achieved, level with the lower planets and the superior vapours of the universe, and he looked forward quite happily to Wednesday afternoon. He recognized no absurdity in the proportion of his wishes; Lyonnesse was the inevitable valley which lay folded among these altitudes. It waited for him, drenched in light like honey from the broken clouds.

It was the only kingdom of the earth which appeared valuable to one who hovered upon wings of air, with an eagle's prerogative of choice in descending. The continents were spread before his eyes; Europe enamelled green, veined with the branching silver of rivers, embossed with a blue tracery of hills; Asia a mysterious colour like smoke, with fringes of brilliance and crystal spears of mountains; Africa wearing a bright disguise of lion skins clasped by a sapphire chain, and the breadth of America like roughened gold stretched between ribs of granite and enriched by the transparent blood of streams. He had travelled over the painted variations of this globe, whose curves sloped upward into a sky of reversed phantoms. Mirage had led him on and a pack of illusions had dogged his footsteps. Mr. Hazard was tired of distances; the small kingdom of Lyonnesse invited him. This valley kingdom, circumscribed and unperilous, gentle in its limitations, was a cure for his soul's vertigo. He surveyed it from the third act of his lyrical drama, and thought it a fit inheritance for his soul. He had no use for larger realms; if he should fall asleep in this valley, if he should fall asleep or die, Lyonnesse was a soft bed and a sweetly scented coffin. Say that from these heights it looked no wider than a grave spangled and plumed with summer grass, and you had said the sum of his desires.

He trusted Clara; even if he had been tempted to ask her for some rare and intricate indulgence he would have had faith in her charity. Knowing the ascetic measure of his appetites, he was doubly certain that she would not let him starve; crisp drops of spring water and spare and wholesome crusts could never be denied him. A long hour on the river once a week; a cup of tea on the terrace now and again when his head ached and Gravelow was a town beleaguered by evil; so much she was sure to give him, and he would ask for no more.

"Next summer you must bring your wife and Lionel," she had said to him; the light modulations of her voice had made music of the words and a sunny mirror for their sense. A delicately flattered picture had appeared, wherein Lionel and his mother smiled kindly upon Mr. Hazard, loving him, approving him, believing him. Mr. Hazard had agreed with Clara; a succession of Junes seemed to promise friendship and peace. Lionel and his mother could not fail to be happy here; Clara's voice made this assurance plain.

Now, as Mr. Hazard surveyed the hope of Wednesday afternoon from the calm summit of accomplishment, he was aware of a strict and exquisite proportion in his felicity. It was fairly divided into halves between the knowledge that he had carved a masterpiece out of the very air of heaven and the knowledge that in two days' time he might follow the level Thames to Lyonnesse. He did not smile or dream of smiling to compare such equal joys.

Gravelow was a beleaguered town tonight, but the hosts encamped upon the surrounding water-meadows were excellent spirits, armies of virtue and benevolence; their banners turned the sky into a field of lilies. These shapes of radiance filled the spaces of the wind blowing from the river; they entered the town and walked in light along its streets; they ascended the stairs of Mr. Hazard's lodgings and knocked invisibly upon his door.

"This," said Mr. Hazard to himself, "is your only secular trap for the soul. These spirits move among temporal matters in serenity and wisdom, but they are repelled by desperation. The violence of my longing drove them from me; they fled from the spectacle of my pain. Now that I am happy they come to me of their own accord; they are like angelic moths and may-flies, and he who would attract them must first kindle a taper. I have Clara and her children to thank for these admirable ghosts."

Tired by his conversation with himself and by certain metaphysical problems presented by those features of heaven perceptible from his window, Mr. Hazard fell asleep before the cocks began to crow. When he awoke, the spiritual hosts had disappeared from the water-meadows, but the scattered clouds revealed enough of gold and jacinth to attest their existence in other spheres.

2

Wasps in the Jam

THE week rushed to its happy ending, swept onward by the triumphant speed of Mr. Hazard's third act. The morning of the seventh day was variable and pale; flashes of cool sunshine ran between the articulations of the rain like little fishes in a vast silvery net. It was impossible to foretell the weather, but all weathers are sanctified by such happiness as Mr. Hazard's, and he could not believe that the sky would not clear as soon as he had turned his face towards the east. He walked over the hollow plain and under dripping trees where the road curved up the hill and down again into the valley before his faith was vindicated. An oriel of blue opened overhead, permitting the suave light of afternoon to colour the falling raindrops. Mr. Hazard was wet to the skin by the time he reached Lyonnesse, but the oriel had widened to a great rose-window through which he beheld the sun above his left shoulder.

Mr. Hazard's sense of victory over a heaven of the mind and a more desirable earth lying at the turn of this narrow lane lent rapidity to his stride; it was unable to efface the lines of worry and fatigue from his brow or to stain his bleached and faded body with its original brightness. In the last month he had unlearnt every lesson of distrust wherein his pride had long and bitterly instructed him, but the marks of that distrustful pride were still visible upon his brow. He felt secure and strong and invulnerable; the third act of his drama was like a harnessed mountain moving under him. Nevertheless he did not look in the least like a man who has subdued a mountain by incomparable powers of will; he looked like a man who has forgotten to eat seven sensible dinners in seven days, and who has been wet to the skin on a chilly June evening. He looked ill and exhausted; his felicity was unapparent, but it was plain that one of his shoes wanted mending, and that there were several buttons missing from his coat.

To Mr. Hodge he seemed a horrid apparition. Mr. Hodge was incapable of that flight of fancy which should liken him to a man hanged in chains or a blanched anatomy rejected by the sea, but the blurred shadows of these comparisons crossed his mind as Mr. Hazard approached. To Clara Mr. Hazard looked, as always, like a poor black sheep whose fleece is silvered by adversity; Rosa saw him charitably as the Prisoner of Chillon, and Allegra had grown accustomed to her scarecrow.

"An appalling person," said Mr. Hodge to Allegra, who was perched upon the balustrade beside him. She nodded absent-mindedly, knowing that Mr. Hazard could not frighten a single bird from a single cherry-tree.

"Ridiculous creature," said Clara to Rosa. "How very wet he is, poor darling! How has he contrived to be so very wet when we have had nothing but sunshowers?"

"You are late," said Clara to Mr. Hazard, with the slight comment of her smile, "but it doesn't matter; we have decided not to try the river today. Allegra has a new sash, or Rosa has curled her hair, or Mr. Hodge prefers to eat his lamb and green peas comfortably hot. I hope you are not too cruelly disappointed; of course you will have a far better dinner indoors, but I know you have a passion for picnics. And now I wonder what in the name of common sense I am to do with you."

"To do with me?" said Mr. Hazard, like a bewildered echo. "Must you do anything with me in the name of common sense?"

"To keep you from catching cold; don't you realize that you are in imminent danger of catching cold? You have swum the Thames in a fit of abstraction, and now you must ask Mr. Hodge to lend you some of his nice new clothes to wear while yours are drying."

"Of course," said Mr. Hodge without looking up. "Please; you must, of course." He tried to speak pleasantly. The attempt was a signal failure; Mr. Hodge was annoyed because Clara had called his clothes nice and new, and his antipathy to Mr. Hazard was dull and sullen, like a bruise upon his mind.

"Thank you," said Mr. Hazard, "you are very kind. But I beg you not to trouble about me; I am not really wet; the sun will dry me in a minute or two."

"I never catch cold," said Mr. Hazard to Clara, sitting down upon the stone balustrade of the terrace. He folded his arms tightly across his ribs and gritted his teeth; by a severe effort of the will he kept himself from shivering. His elbows pressed his clenched fists into his ribs, and the shudder passed from his bones obediently as his will directed.

"So I perceive," said Clara with a delicate flavour of malice in her voice. "It's not at all clever of you to refuse my good advice, but I see that you are past praying for. When you sneeze, I shan't even bother to say: 'God bless you.' But of course you won't sneeze; you're much too stubborn to sneeze."

"Mr. Hodge has a beautiful bottle-green coat," said Allegra, "with brass buttons; he's particularly proud of the brass buttons. You'd far better borrow it."

"But your shoes," said Rosa. "At least be reasonable about your shoes. . . ."

"It's quite hopeless, my dears," said Clara, "don't torment him; he must be allowed to catch his own colds in peace. It is almost dinner-time, and the boys have disappeared; will somebody please go hunt for them?"

"I will," said Mr. Hodge, jumping from his seat. His solid step went quickly down the path. He hunched his broad shoulders, shrugging a burden from his mind; he was relieved to be rid of Mr. Hazard's company, and he whistled as he went.

3

Dry Bread and Radishes

MR. HAZARD had worn his shabbiest coat for the picnic, the same coat which had received such cruel usage at the hands of Omar Vrioni's troops during the fighting at Distomo in February 1827. It was a shocking coat; the celebrated bandit Polinario, meeting Mr. Hazard in the autumn of 1831 upon the solitary road between Madrilejos and Puerto Lapiche, had grinned compassionately at the rents in its lining and returned it to its owner with a courtly bow. Mr. Hazard had refused the robber's offer of a sheepskin jacket; he was fond of the coat, which had been made by an Athenian tailor in 1825. Tonight it was undoubtedly wet, but it had been wetter at Mauritius, in the hurricane of 1828; the *coup de vent* which had wrecked the East-Indiaman *George Canning* had blown away at least one of its buttons. It had seemed a suitable garment in which to study the condition of Mr. Telfair's slaves, but it was a curious blot upon the argent shield of Clara's dinnertable.

Clara intended to have the panelling tinted cream-colour as soon as she went north in August; she had never liked the cold pearly grey of its paint. This evening, however, she was well pleased with the look of the room; there was a glimmering play of rainbows upon the walls, and a faint reflected pattern of leaves and clouds touched with a counterfeited light. Her children's faces shone clear and fragile as four crescents set above the oval board. It was that lovely hour which preserves an equable balance between sunset and the radiance of the moon; the children's faces were rosy against the cold pearl-coloured walls and the greenish glass of the window-panes. Their small faces, sharply carven, elfin and aquiline, shone rosy and freckled with gold in the light from the west.

"The translucid, or diaphane," said Mr. Hazard to Clara. " 'The sun is its father, the moon is its mother.' The dogma of Hermes Trismegistus."

Clara nodded indulgently, hoping that he would drink his soup while it was hot and that the rain water dripping from his clothes would not stain the delicate beasts and flowers of the

Persian rug. She glanced at Mr. Hodge, aware of an acrid breath of intolerance in the crystalline air about her. Mr. Hodge appeared sedate and personable in his dark-blue coat; his nankeen trousers were neatly strapped under shapely and well-polished insteps. He was listening to Tristram's agreeable persiflage; only the corner of his lowered eye swerved suspiciously towards Mr. Hazard's last words.

"I wish the absurd creature would not choose this occasion upon which to talk transcendental folly," said Clara to herself. "He is doing it quite idly, to keep his teeth from chattering; he does not care tuppence for his athanors, elixirs, and pantacles. He is afraid he will have a chill if he admits he is human, and so he talks about Paracelsus and sidereal phantoms."

Perhaps Mr. Hazard was possessed of a nervous organism so sensitive that Clara's thought disturbed it like a command; perhaps he fell silent for some other reason. To Clara's relief he spoke no further word save in answer to the circumspect urbanity of her own conversation, which avoided hermetic pitfalls by a feminine magic peculiar to itself. Nobody else paid the slightest heed to Mr. Hazard; he sat eating bread and radishes, and staring at the children as if he had never seen them before. It was true that he had never seen the boys before, yet he looked oftener at Allegra. When he looked at Tristram and Hilary, he saw that Hilary was grave and regular as a golden coin, but that Tristram was harder to capture or apprehend by even the quickest senses. He was so volatile an essence that he escaped definition; Mr. Hazard admired his fiery and lively grace and the exquisite impudence of his bearing.

Either by accident or design, Mr. Hazard drank his soup while it was hot, and felt much recovered. He was now beyond the petty malice of a physical chill, and it had not yet occurred to him that the surrounding atmosphere contained a frigid element of antipathy. His quick susceptive wits were away upon an argosy of wool-gathering, or their burning course was benumbed by cold or stayed and averted by some alien spell. It was strange that the unfortunate Mr. Hazard should remain unmoved; it was stranger that the high-spirited Mr. Hazard should remain submissive; it was strangest that the proud and suspicious Mr. Hazard should remain unaware of an inimical humour. Nevertheless he so remained; Clara had mixed forgetfulness among her innumerable charms.

Presently Mr. Hodge's eyes swerved under lowered lids and rested for a second time upon Mr. Hazard; Mr. Hodge removed his eyes from Mr. Hazard's face as hastily as if they had been the horns of a snail brought into alarming contact with evil. He looked at Mr. Hazard's plate and looked away again in anger and contempt.

"He is eating salt with his bread like a fool, and buttering his radishes like a Frenchman," said Mr. Hodge to himself with energy. "A man who eats salt with his bread and butters his radishes is a loathsome phenomenon; I wonder that Lady Clara permits such a fellow at her table."

"I am afraid that Mr. Hodge is not liking poor Mr. Hazard," said Clara to herself. "It is a pity that there is so much prejudice in the world. I wonder whether I shall be able to reconcile their chemical differences; Lyonnesse is not the place for explosions. It was bound to happen sooner or later, I suppose, but I hope for poor Mr. Hazard's sake that I can postpone the inevitable."

"We will have tea on the terrace, children," said Clara in her clear unhurried voice, rising from the table in a rustle of India muslin.

4

Unsubstantial Pageant Faded

ALTHOUGH Clara was cast in a porcelain mould, she was both liberal and humane. Her mind was temperate and well-bred; the sentimental and the intolerant were alike ludicrous in her sight. She was the calm sophisticated foe of cruelties and oppressions; if Kandler of the Albrechtsburg had ever elected to use the Samothracian Victory as a model for one of his life-size china ladies, his creation might have been Clara's double. She wore no cockades; her loyalties were not confessed by so much as a red or a white rose. She smiled, forgiving a rude variety of foibles; she sprinkled attar of bergamot upon factions and the tides of party strife. Of course she was heartily in favour of reform; her father had been known to be a Whig, her husband was said to be a rebel.

Nevertheless if the Duke of Wellington or Sir Robert Peel sat next to her at dinner, she could not help feeling a gentle pity for the opposition, and she remembered that Lord Camphile had never approved of Mr. Macaulay.

Her father's firm opinions were still an article of faith for her, but her lighter and more flexible brain had altered them from a political decalogue into a set of pleasant sympathies. She was indifferent to Don Pedro and Don Miguel; she felt a moderate interest in the tea monopoly, and she was truly concerned that the Negroes must still submit to the cart-whip. She was a brilliant ornament of Lord Grey's routs, and the poor of the parish adored her.

Now it distressed her to witness the harsh disfavour with which Mr. Hodge so evidently regarded Mr. Hazard. Mr. Hodge was valuable to her in more ways than one; she could not ignore his prejudices. Her father had discovered Mr. Hodge; Lord Camphile had recognized the young man's eminent merits, and he had removed him from a desk in Leadenhall Street and exalted him into a private secretary. Mr. Hodge had been the comfort of Lord Camphile's closing years, which declined so fiercely into the grave that his family and friends were shrivelled into nonentities at his bedside. Mr. Hodge's bad manners and excellent abilities had sustained Lord Camphile through the cold fury of dying; no one else could be so admirably offensive to an importunate caller as Mr. Hodge.

Clara had inherited him; Lord Camphile would have preferred to leave him to Geraldine, but Mr. Hodge, who had a certain freedom of choice in the matter, had selected Clara from the beginning. Clara was the one Circe who had ever won him from his determined policy of rudeness; her long throat, her small and arrogant head with its coronet of gilded bronze, the lucent jewels of her eyes, formed a type of perfection for Mr. Hodge. Mr. Hodge had been a sceptic and a materialist ever since he was breeched; Clara was his first religion, and his devout novitiate was not yet ended.

He had not presumed to fall in love with her; she would never have permitted such an emotion to mar the deference of his attitude. He, whose habitual gesture towards the world was too discourteous to record, was on his knees to Clara. She was seven years his senior; in the grim secrecy of his soul he acknowledged her seven generations his better. He gloried in his subservience, and as he crushed the timid and the vain in his invincible progress towards success, he brought their limp bodies to Clara and laid them upon her altar like the spoils of war. She was often grieved by these pitiful trophies; this evening she was deeply grieved by his implied scorn for Mr. Hazard.

"He must not be allowed to hurt people's feelings," said Clara to Rosa. "Do you think Mr. Hazard has noticed a slight lack of cordiality, my love? It is very distressing to be present upon these occasions; there is a taint of the slaughter-house about the whole proceeding which is not to my taste. I must scold Hodge unmercifully as soon as Mr. Hazard goes home."

"I don't think Mr. Hazard has noticed anything as yet, Mama," said Rosa soothingly, "of course it's dreadfully evident to us, but Mr. Hazard is so very absent-minded, and he has been listening to Tristram and watching Allegra, and I really believe he is happy. He is always rather quiet, isn't he, when other people are talking? Perhaps he is tired, or has a headache, or has received bad news in a letter from Spain; perhaps he is only having trouble with Job. I truly don't think he has noticed anything amiss."

"I hope with all my heart that he has not," said Clara plaintively. "He is such a defenceless person, such a parcel of absurd sensibilities. But I don't want his feelings to be hurt; I wish he would go home. Is he looking more than usually ill, or is that simply a nervous imagination upon my part?"

"He always looks rather—well, you know the way he always looks, Mama," said Rosa. "Perhaps he does look a little less well than usual, but then he never looks very well."

"Heigh-ho," said Clara, "I suppose you are right, my dear. It's silly to worry about trifles; it spoils the complexion. But one does rather, about poor Mr. Hazard."

"One does," said Rosa, whose heart was soft for the unlucky.

The wind had fallen, with the subsiding rain, and now the evening was clear and warm; light strained through a thin fleece of clouds lay purified and distilled into dewdrops among the grass. Two great chairs curved and fluted like sea-shells stood upon the terrace; Clara sat in one, but the other was empty, since everyone else sat upon the balustrade. The empty chair, varnished in the several tints of nacre, was brim-full of green reflections. It was a chair for a naiad, and Mr. Hazard wished that Allegra might be persuaded to pause there for a moment. Yet to see her running down the path, as she was sure to do in the next moment, was as good or better; in the purified light she would fly like a swallow, swoop like a silver bat, be off into nothingness like the shadow of a cloud. Meanwhile the present interposed a globe of pearl between Mr. Hazard and his fate.

5

Crack of Doom in a Teacup

MR. HAZARD had noticed so little that he was still happy. He had no desire to talk, but his silence was neither despondent nor afraid. He did as he pleased, sitting in a fair degree of comfort upon the balustrade, with his back against a marble urn. The marble urn was cold, and velvety with moss. He listened to Tristram, convinced that he smiled; he said: "Hah" in his brief new fashion of laughing, for the aerial performances of Tristram's wit were greatly to his mind. He watched Allegra, and had no quarrel with the universe which wheeled about her planet. His own sphere swung unguided in the hollow sky above them.

"How can he be so deaf, with that look of dismaying intelligence?" Clara asked herself resignedly. "Or so blind, with those preternatural eyes upon their faces? He is under a sleep-walking enchantment, but Hodge will wake him in a minute like the crack of doom."

Clara had wrapped her smooth shoulders in a violet scarf with bands of swan's-down along its edges; she felt a vague tremor of sorrow, which she mistook for the cool night wind, and she muffled her throat in the soft scarf and drew back into the depths of her chair. She had an irrelevant impulse to pray for Mr. Hazard's soul.

It was Rosa's courteous pity which shattered

the crystal instant; she could not bear Mr. Hazard to suffer neglect, and to her glittering childish vision he appeared a tragic skeleton, a creature stripped of the bare necessities of joy. She cast about in the bright pool of her memory for consolation or praise.

"Have you finished your sonnet to Milton, Mr. Hazard?" asked Rosa; her voice was distinct and sweet as a bird's in the twilight.

Tristram stopped talking and looked at Mr. Hazard; he was surprised, but lenient and amused, as befitted his nature. Hilary was too polite and Allegra too careless even to glance in Mr. Hazard's direction; they turned the pages of a book of Flaxman drawings and laughed between themselves. Mr. Hodge stared straight at Mr. Hazard; his patience was at an end. He lowered his eyes as if he had stared at a nameless serpent, and spoke.

"Poor Milton," said Mr. Hodge in his heavy mysterious voice, which was yet plain enough for his meaning.

Mr. Hazard recognized the crack of doom; he could not believe his senses. He was startled as he had been startled at the Hartleighs' breakfast-table upon the first morning of his influenza; the crystal instant was shattered, his nerves sustained the shock of an actual blow. By a violent exertion of his powers of self-command he reassumed his tranquillity; not his least eyelash or the smallest muscle of his face had betrayed him. Mr. Hodge was vexed by this apparent calm; he doubted whether Mr. Hazard had understood him, and he cursed the other for a blockhead and a fool.

Mr. Hodge did not suspect the truth. Mr. Hazard matched his will against the inimical will of Mr. Hodge, and at the cost of unmeasured spiritual energy he preserved the victory to himself. The truth, however, would have given the liveliest satisfaction to Mr. Hodge had he but known it. Behind the puny shield of his breastbone Mr. Hazard's heart paused in horror, knocked three times like a frantic prisoner, and went forward haltingly, as if its pulse were lamed. On the 13th of May, in Cold-bath Fields, a member of the Metropolitan police force had struck Mr. Hazard a smart blow with his stick; the blow had fallen with sickening impact upon Mr. Hazard's left temple, but it had caused him far less inconvenience than Mr. Hodge's words were now causing him. The strokes were similar, but Mr. Hodge's was the shrewder onslaught, and far more venomous in its effects.

Like execrable hebenon the poison entered Mr. Hazard's brain and was mixed into his blood and the marrow of his bones with immediate virulence. It was hatred, simple hatred, that rank poison fatal to Mr. Hazard's health, which now plagued his veins.

The constable had not hated Mr. Hazard, nor had his truncheon been doctored with contagion. Mr. Hazard was a bystander in Cold-bath Fields, a bystander as innocent as an embittered revolutionary can ever hope to be. The blow was a brisk reminder to move on, and so soon as his giddiness would permit, Mr. Hazard had moved on with the dispersing crowd. Nothing rankled within the cut on his forehead; a square of court-plaster covered it with oblivion. Mr. Hodge's words inflicted a severer wound; the three heavy syllables were pointed with hatred. Mr. Hazard knew hatred when he heard it, and the knowledge wrought no good in him.

There was that in Mr. Hazard's soul, tenable as strength or weakness, which considered the most ungenial theory with scrupulous faith. Above the anger and amazement which dissolved his joints his stricter intellect examined Mr. Hodge's words by its rational light. Was it possible that the sacred name of Milton was dishonoured in the sonnet which Mr. Hazard had written, or, more largely, was there anything in the obscurest corner of Mr. Hazard's spirit which rendered him unfit to celebrate this name in verse? Even as he sat wickedly entranced by hatred, even as his heart was stifled in his side, he considered very gravely whether or not he had done wrong.

The moment passed; only Mr. Hodge and Mr. Hazard were aware that such a moment had ticked sullenly upon the moonlight dial of the hour. Mr. Hodge was disappointed; Mr. Hazard was sensible of a profound fatigue. The moment's dull assault had shaken him, but now emotion and thought were gone from him and he cared not whether he fainted or fell asleep or died, if only he need not answer Mr. Hodge.

Mr. Hazard neither fainted nor fell asleep; a trivial hope had died within him, perishing between the limping pulses of his heart. He might possibly have chosen to die with it had he been given any choice in the matter, but the slight machinery of his flesh was not so simply stilled. It was too vital to be murdered outright by a diminished flow of happiness; it was accustomed to a more stringent diet than the honeyed fancies with which Clara had nurtured it for a while. Mr. Hazard realized for the thousandth time that it is difficult to die of that sharp and fugitive pang which is commonly miscalled a broken heart.

This pang may be inflicted by the most unimportant means; let it not be held a special folly upon the part of Mr. Hazard that he now experienced this pang. Mr. Hazard was conversant with many dead and living tongues, and it was his misfortune that among these none was more familiar to his ears than the forked vocabulary of hatred. He translated Mr. Hodge's two words with accurate skill; they informed him that he was an appalling person, unfit to associate with the innocent and the noble, that his appearance was odd, his principles outrageous, and his opinions contemptible. Their ten laconic letters told him that he was at all points detestable to Mr. Hodge. The lovely grave which was prepared for him in the valley of Lyonnesse was no longer his own; Mr. Hodge had filled it with the rotten body of the past.

Mr. Hazard's extreme fatigue followed upon this knowledge; the rigours of his late triumph over the mountains and the archangelic monsters of his brain had wearied him, but the last moment had tried his endurance by a harder proof. So short a space of clockwork time lay between Rosa's artless question and his answer that to the child the pause was unapparent.

"I have not finished the sonnet yet," said Mr. Hazard, "but I shall finish it tonight, and if I am to finish it tonight, I fear I must go home. Good-night, Lady Clara; I shall heed your excellent advice and go home. Good-night, little Rosa; Allegra, good-night."

Mr. Hazard, who was determined to finish the sonnet before he fell asleep, walked swiftly back to Gravelow along a narrow path cut from another world. He trod delicately, keeping his eyes upon the narrow path, stepping with infinite care over clustered shadows. On either side of him there bloomed a fresh profusion of weeds, festooned and knotted into walls which hid the sky and flourished wantonly with evil. Mr. Hazard looked neither to left nor to right, and as he walked, he strove to remember no words in the two worlds except the octave of his own sonnet to Milton.

6

Portrait of a Natural Force

"Obviously," said Mr. Hodge, "I cannot pretend to say what Sir John would think on the subject."

"Obviously you cannot," Clara told him with her most mischievous smile.

"But," continued Mr. Hodge, ignoring the snub, "I can tell you precisely what Lord Camphile would have thought. Your father would have considered this person a thoroughly undesirable acquaintance; such a person could never have crossed the threshold of your father's house."

"You are amazingly cool to lecture me, Hodge," said Clara. "And of course Papa was a horrid martinet in such matters. Poor Mr. Hazard is quite harmless, and you must admit that he is a gentleman. The children are really fond of him."

"I admit nothing of the sort," said Mr. Hodge. "On the contrary, I deny it flatly; Mr. Hazard does not fulfil my notion of a gentleman. But then, as you are aware, I am no judge."

"Don't be tiresome," said Clara. "I shall not give you the satisfaction of understanding you."

"Very well," said Mr. Hodge. "Now, as to the children, that is the most serious part of the business. I may appear cool when I lecture you, but, believe me, I am anything but cool; my blood boils to behold this man the companion of your children. You are a woman of the world, and as such protected against his influence; Rosa and Allegra are children, malleable as yet, innocent and unformed. He may impress their minds most dangerously."

"My dear Hodge," said Clara gaily, "have you seen them together? The girls patronize poor Mr. Hazard in the most outrageous manner; they laugh at his verse, his conversation, and the fashion of his cravats. It is very wrong, to be sure, but it relieves my mind of all anxiety concerning their malleable natures. They are a pair of minxes, and they regard poor Mr. Hazard as a cause for mirth. He will forgive them anything under heaven, but sometimes they drive him out of his wits with their teasing."

"Out of his wits!" cried Mr. Hodge. "That he is, and has always been; the man is mad. I could tell you a story or two of his school-days which you would not care to repeat to Tristram and Hilary. You know the disgraceful farce of his career at the University, but he was always a *mauvais sujet*, a pestilential player to the gallery. There is a sour hysteria in his make-up which is worse than positive crime. Not that he has always stopped short of crime, by certain credible reports; he has even advocated . . ."

"Never mind that juvenile nonsense," said Clara, "I dare say he was an uncommonly silly boy, but there is not an ounce of harm in the poor creature. I have tied him into a true-love knot round my little finger; if I took the trouble, I could quite easily turn him into a churchwarden and a justice of the peace."

"Your true-lover's knot is an asp," said Mr. Hodge. "He will but sting you for your pains."

"How poetic you are," said Clara, "and how illiberal! I thought you were a red-hot radical; Papa used always to laugh at your Jacobin rubbish, as he called it."

"I am a liberal," said Mr. Hodge sullenly, "but not a latitudinarian. I am a friend of liberty, but not a licenser of libertines. It was an ill day for freedom when Mr. Hazard sheltered his iniquities beneath her cloak; he is a born seducer, and he prostitutes the cause that he espouses."

"You talk like a nonconformist," said Clara, "but I believe you were, before you won your tripos and became a reformer. Please don't reform Mr. Hazard; your account of him is charmingly romantic. I wish he would fall in love with me, but I fear he has a humble admiration for that mocking Artemis, Allegra, who does nothing but flout him."

"You are very frivolous, Lady Clara," said Mr. Hodge, frowning heavily at a lunar moth.

"I marvel that you can make a jest of this man's scandalous history. I suppose you are the fittest judge of your daughters' associates, and that I am impertinent in suggesting . . ."

"I am," said Clara with composure, "and you are excessively impertinent to advise me, my dear Hodge. Nevertheless I shall overlook it, because of my promise to Papa that no one but you should teach the boys mathematics. Though why the poor lambs must learn mathematics . . ."

"Mental discipline," said Mr. Hodge, "a control to which Mr. Hazard has never submitted his weakly rebellious brain. He is ignorant in the worst sense; misguided, ill-conditioned, ungovernable. He is a disastrous model for the boys."

"But he has most agreeable manners," said Clara. "Eccentric, perhaps, but agreeable, and delightfully self-effacing. I repeat, the poor creature is a gentleman. He has led a miserable life out of his proper *milieu;* his folly has been punished by an inferno of underbred bluestockings and shoddy philosophers. His pleasure in our company is pathetic to witness. I have not the heart to cast him off as his family did."

Portrait of a Natural Force

"Did you know that his scoundrelly old grandfather was born in America?" asked Mr. Hodge. "It has become a parrot-cry among his cockney friends to say that the fellow's blood is respectable if not distinguished, but his grandfather was an unscrupulous ruffian, a lucky adventurer. Your Mr. Hazard is thoroughly un-English; he is the typical malcontent. You have only to look at his hat . . ."

"To see that he has not a penny, Hodge," said Clara quickly. "He has not inherited his grandfather's talents; he is a very unlucky adventurer. His conscience is an instrument of torture; he cannot take a step without a scruple, and yet he is for ever taking new steps. And of course he is fanatically honest; you see his honesty in his eyes."

"I see nothing of the sort," said Mr. Hodge. "Forgive my plain-speaking, which you may prefer to call rudeness, but I see insanity in his eyes, and violence, and a base surrender to despair. Do not talk to me of the look in his eyes, Lady Clara, or I shall be thinking of strait jackets at once."

"Ah, you are too unkind," said Clara with a

sigh, "you are cruel, Hodge; why must you hate him so bitterly? He is ill; he is broken by life. He would never forgive me for saying this, but it must be clear to everyone who sees him. He is profoundly unhappy; have you not enough happiness of your own to be able to spare him a crumb from my table?"

"No," said Mr. Hodge, looking square into Clara's blue eyes, which were brilliant with tears, "no; frankly, no, since you ask me. I have not a tithe of the happiness I desire; nor shall I have it this side the grave. But I do not intend to share my crumbs with Mr. Hazard."

Clara was not flattered by this profession; she thought it indecorous and unbecoming upon the part of her sons' tutor. At the same time she was perfectly capable of forgiving it; she blinked her lovely eyes once, and considered it unsaid. Mr. Hodge was a masterly teacher of mathematics, and far cleverer than any agent in the management of her affairs. Her father had convinced her of his worth; his Cambridge honours and the esteem in which the Company had held him proved his practical ability. She blinked her eyes and was blind when he offended; she knew she could frighten him by lifting her eyebrows by the fraction of an inch. She was satisfied that he should adore her instead of one of her daughters; it might have been awkward if he had adored Rosa or Allegra. About Clara he could nurse no illusions, but if he loved Rosa or Allegra he might dare to reckon up his chances. Mr. Hodge was no bewildered dreamer, to be content with visions. He looked very discontented indeed as he sat with his eyes on the ground.

"'Fallings from us, vanishings; blank misgivings of a creature moving about in worlds not realized ...'" said Clara, thinking of poor Mr. Hazard.

"Does he teach you metaphysical poetry?" asked Mr. Hodge savagely. "I have the *Revue des deux mondes* in my pocket, with Musset's new play in it, but you won't care about Marianne's caprices now that you have taken to quoting Wordsworth."

Clara looked at Mr. Hodge; in the airy moonlight he appeared solid and well-proportioned, tall and muscular, and handsome in a heavy way of his own. His prosperity shone from his coat buttons and from the richer seals upon his watch chain. He scowled, but it was evident that he was a successful person.

"You mustn't be cruel, Hodge," said Clara firmly. "Good-night; you must read the thirteenth chapter of Corinthians and pray for charity. You will have to learn to share your crumbs with Mr. Hazard; I cannot let anyone starve upon my door-step. And he is hungrier than you, although he will never admit it. Remember, you must learn to share your crumbs."

"Must I?" asked Mr. Hodge, as she left him in the moonlight. "Must I indeed? I wonder." His voice was weighty with mysteries and projects. Presently he stopped scowling and strolled along the path by the river-bank, whistling between his strong white teeth.

"'*Moi, pour un peu d'amour je donnerais mes jours,
    Et je les donnerais pour rien sans les amours*',"

whistled Mr. Hodge in the airy moonlight.

Mr. Hodge, also, was a dreamer after his own fashion; he was not content with visions, yet he too indulged a secret phantasmagoria of hope. Strange things had come to pass; a clerk in the East India Company had been made private secretary to Lord Camphile, and people had been known to die, even in Persia. There was no reason why Mr. Hodge should permit a stumbling-block to lie across his path. He kicked a pebble from his path, and it fell into the river, leaving a faint agitation of ripples to widen under the moon.

7

Tiptoe on a Tombstone

IT was Susan's invariable rule to bring Mr. Hazard a cup of tea when she waked him at seven o'clock. Susan was a servant in the employ of Mr. Hazard's landlady; she was both virtuous and tender-hearted, and she had come to feel a loyal and benevolent affection for the eccentric lodger. Susan was nineteen years old, a tall fresh-coloured girl with an excessive quantity of reddish hair bundled under her mob-cap. The burning innocence of her eyes was shadowed by a starched ruffle, and the strength and litheness of her limbs were inconspicuous in pink and lavender prints.

It was the rustle of these stiffened skirts which waked Mr. Hazard every morning; the curtain-rings played a jangling tune, the day drove a broad wedge of light into the room, and Susan set the little tea-tray down with a clatter within six inches of Mr. Hazard's head. By the time he had moved his head upon the pillow she had disappeared beyond the brisk click of the door. The tea soothed Mr. Hazard more slowly than Susan had roused him; it revived him with leisurely warmth. The two slices of bread and butter looked no more edible than the fringed napkin under them, but the tea was welcome.

It was Susan's private conviction that Mr. Hazard was in grave danger of dying. In the first place, she believed him to be at least fifty, and in Susan's opinion fifty was not an unsuitable age at which to die. In the second place, she had seldom, if ever, seen anyone so thin as Mr. Hazard, and she observed with misgivings that the harder Mr. Hazard worked, the less he appeared to care for cutlets and potatoes. In the third place, and at this point Susan trembled as if her small felt slippers had advanced noiselessly into a churchyard, the sharp implacable morning, driving its rigid beam of light into the room, revealed Mr. Hazard laid asleep in such pallor and apathy as Susan had never beheld upon the pillow of a living man. It was her deep unspoken pride that each day she waked him, not from slumber, but from the stealthy approach of death. She let the curtain-rings jingle in merry discord; she set down the tea-tray with deliberate clatter of spoons and bent her childish face above Mr. Hazard for an instant, to make sure that he lived.

Each day she had succeeded in waking him; she was beginning to be confident that so long as she carried a cup of tea to him every morning at seven o'clock, he could not die. It was not difficult to wake him; Mr. Hazard was a light sleeper, and the window shone full upon his eyelids. In cold rainy reflections or in the richer colours of sun Susan bent her face above Mr. Hazard's pillow and, assured that he lived, shut the door joyfully upon her miracle.

Today she was not so certain; he did not move, although his eyes looked past her to the window, and past the window to the sky. Susan was all at once afraid; she went from the room without a backward glance, stepping as if she tip-toed across a grave. She closed the door softly, and then leaned against it, trembling until her starched apron rustled like leaves in the wind. In her crisp apron and pink print gown she trem-bled and shook like a tall young tree of laurel. She had not known, before she felt this sudden fear, how very fond she was of Mr. Hazard.

Mr. Hazard was alive, alive at first to a vague foreknowledge of evil, which broke in clear disas-ter over his mind, as the curtains were divided by the day, and left no smallest cloud upon his mem-ory. He was unaware of Susan's presence; he closed his eyes again in a futile attempt to tem-per the unmerciful light to his mind. The light beat upon his pillow with a force like noise and sensible violence; he interposed the thin and insuf-ficient tissue of his eyelids between his memory and the full radiance of morning, and it seemed to him that his eyelids cast no shadow upon his eyes or upon the memory behind them. He felt that the bones of his forehead were fragile and transparent under the light, and he wished that he lay asleep on the averted surface of the earth which was turned away from the sun and cool in the shadow of itself.

The feathers in Mr. Hazard's pillow were reassembled into wings; for a moment they bore him dizzily toward the sun. He had no power over their flight, which refused to turn westward into shadow or eastward into the valley of Lyonnesse. Their flight was straight toward the sun, and then that vast supremacy of fire melted the petty ligaments which bound the wings together, and they parted in mid-air and fell lightly back to the place from whence they came. Mr. Hazard fell heavily, head downward, without sense or power. It was a relief to him to find that he still lay upon his own bed in Gravelow; the feathers of his pillow were quiet within a linen pillow-case, and his mind was stunned into quiet within the transparent bones of his skull.

Mr. Hazard looked at the cup of tea which Susan had left by his bed; he wondered how it had been conveyed there, for he had no recollection of Susan's visit. Then he knew that the girl had come and gone, because there was the cup of tea upon the table, and the curtains flung wide to admit the sunlight. Mr. Hazard did not drink the tea, although he was somewhat thirsty; he pulled the curtains across the window and vainly imagined that he might sleep again. He could neither fly nor crawl into that cone of shadow cast by the earth, but he could make a little shadow of his own with three yards of faded cotton strung upon jingling rings.

Mr. Hazard did not sleep again that morning; in half an hour he arose and bathed and dressed. He pushed back the curtains impatiently and wished he could push back the walls of the house; he recognized the futility of evading the light. The sweet air entered with the light, not cruel, not sharp as a knife at his temple, but cool as spring water or dissolving snow. It was worse than useless to cower in an obscure cave of darkness while the air flowed with the suave freedom of the sea round the margins of sense and understanding. The pure air permeated the marrow of his bones, and his heart leaned upon its waves and was upheld in safety.

Mr. Hazard saw his tragedy in its true proportions; he realized the unimportance of his grief. Like every other mortal who remembers his childhood, he carried at the back of his brain a memory of soap-bubbles, of the clean pipe sticking to his lips, the pipe which was intended for a man, but whose fate it was to be broken between the hot fingers of a child, the taste of soap-suds in his mouth, and the vision of the hollow globes created out of childish breath and a basin of cloudy water, floating upward with the tints of a pigeon's wing upon their curves, melting in light against a sapphire sky. His grief had all the qualities of a soap-bubble, the impermanence and blown perfection of that flower of the atmosphere. Only, while its single leaf survived, it had appeared a type of universal happiness, and with its blossom fallen to less than smoke, to less than a drop of dew, it retained the shape of heaven.

Mr. Hazard sat by the open window; the sunlight moved a slanting finger across the pages of his book. "God will not withdraw his anger; the very helpers of the sea-dragon crouch under him." The book was the Book of Job, the Hebrew Hagiographa. Susan entered with the breakfast tray;

she started as she saw Mr. Hazard surrounded by twenty volumes, their pages ruffled by the sunny wind. She looked at Mr. Hazard, and only the living mirrors of his eyes assured her that he had not died.

"But you have not drunk your tea, sir," said Susan. "You are alive, but you have not drunk your tea. You always drank your tea before to-day."

Mr. Hazard, to whom her language seemed reasonable enough, inclined his head in assent. Susan was horrified by her own words, but to Mr. Hazard they were clear as the Greek characters of the Septuagint. He noticed that her skin was like the lining of a conch-shell and that drops like sea-water lay along its rose.

"I'm sorry about your toast, sir," said Susan. Mr. Hazard looked at the toast, and perceived nothing wrong with it. He did not know that the sorrow in Susan's voice was for him. She was afraid; even the little living images of herself in Mr. Hazard's eyes failed to convince her that the clatter of a teaspoon had waked him at seven o'clock that morning.

8

The Ointment of the Apothecary

IT was an unlucky circumstance for Mr. Hazard that he was not a fool. His mind was a constant traitor to his spirit in its quickness, its coldness, its unpitying and bitter mirth. To enchant this mind to lethargy, to drug it with spiced poppy and to bind its sinews with silk and the plaited strands of womens' hair was no easy matter; Clara had accomplished it because she did not try, because she did not truly care whether or not she succeeded. Mr. Hazard had been grateful to her in proportion to the peace she had conferred upon his spirit. He was of his spirit's party, ever at odds with his own mind; his mind was a scorner, a tyrant, a torturer, and he delighted in any triumph over the enemy. With Clara's help he had kept the clever brute in prison for three months of pastoral holiday, and all the while the creature had slaved for him, performing barbarous labours which his spirit had transformed into this edifice of silver which was piled in foolscap pages under his hand.

Mr. Hodge had unlocked the prison and let

loose the demoniacal mind, and now it sped, a lean and smiling monster, through the high chambers of the soul, splintering the crystal roofs, breaking the looking-glass walls with the vibrations of its laughter. His mind was no friend to Mr. Hazard; his mind was the sworn friend of Mr. Hodge. How swiftly, with what malicious pleasure in the deed, had his mind destroyed the brittle fabric of this dream! Now, retaining still the diminished form of heaven, the dream had escaped him for ever. This brutality his mind had wrought, with the aid and comfort of Mr. Hodge, upon his unsuspecting spirit. Clara, who had kept the key to the dungeon in her embroidered pocket, was miles away at Lyonnesse, sewing a fine seam in stitches like humming-bird's feathers, leaning back against a cushion of grass-green silk, sprinkling sugar in tiny snow-flakes over Mr. Hodge's strawberries.

The toast upon the breakfast tray was burnt, but Mr. Hazard had no appetite for toast and marmalade. He sat in the clean excellence of morning, in the full stream of light and scented air, a gentleman of forty, threadbare, reduced and worn to the structural integrity of the skeleton. The faults and misfortunes of earth and his own flesh, the temporal corrosion of the years, the inward-gnawing tooth of scruple, the stubborn and fanatic impulse of his pride, all these had stripped and bitten Mr. Hazard down to the ultimate framework of himself. He might serve to illustrate either an anatomy lesson or a text from Ecclesiastes. He was a simple pattern of mortality, drawn plain in intellectual black and white upon this summer day.

He sat with folded arms, regarding neither the breakfast tray nor the piles of books beyond it. Such things, set close together upon a table, were worthy to be burned; their level orderly rows annoyed him. Toast in a rack; curled shavings from a flitch of bacon; Fedor Glinka's metrical paraphrase of the Book of Job; a pat of butter embossed with clover leaves; a pair of boiled eggs, pale brown like biscuit porcelain; Eichorn's *Einleitung* and Holmes and Parson's new edition of the Septuagint; a napkin twisted into a cocked hat; a silver jug of milk; a little rose with cream-coloured petals; Kennicott and de Rossi's collation of the Hebrew manuscripts. Such things might have their uses, but for the life of him Mr. Hazard could not remember what he had to do with them. He was bothered by their presence; he thought of ringing for Susan and bidding her remove them from his table.

"I wish," said Mr. Hazard to his mind, "that you would have the common decency to stay where you belong, out of my sight and underground. Must I be for ever driven from pillar to post by your damnable mockery?"

"Out of sight, out of mind," said Mr. Hazard's mind rudely. "From the pillars of the temple to the whipping-post; yes, and back again. Mr. Hodge says you are out of your mind."

"My will subdued you," said Mr. Hazard, "I made you build a lyric tower out of all the tongues of Babel . . ."

"There sits the fellow who built your lyric tower, since you choose to call it by such a flowery name. There sits your immortal soul, Mr. Hazard, on the other side of your breakfast-table, and a precious fool he appears to be. He will make a charming incompetent second in your duel with Mr. Hodge," said Mr. Hazard's mind. "Now, if you would but leave the priming of the pistols to me . . ."

"Be quiet," said Mr. Hazard. "Will you have the goodness to be quiet, and to permit me to finish my breakfast in peace?"

"How can you finish what you haven't yet begun?" asked Mr. Hazard's mind with a hateful smile. "Shall I ring for fresh tea, or do you prefer to go straight on with the fourth act? You should take better care of your health if we are to make the fourth act a worthy successor to the third."

"Do as you please," said Mr. Hazard, "I shall hire a boat and spend the morning on the river. I hope you will not consider it necessary to inflict your company upon me; I am tired, and I wish to be alone."

"Have pity upon that poor fellow over there, and let him go with you," said Mr. Hazard's mind. "If you leave him with me, I shall torment him, and he looks quite unfit for such inhuman treatment. You, my friend, are accustomed to my rough manners, but that fellow with the feathered shoulder-blades is evidently afraid of me."

Mr. Hazard saw his mind distinctly, sitting

= 213 =

in an attitude of negligent grace in the most comfortable chair the room afforded. The mind was attired in black; it wore an air elegant and satirical and seemed forever upon the point of taking snuff. There were no ruffles at its wrists, no sword at its side; it was clothed in a fluttering ambiguity of sable rags, and yet it contrived to suggest, by a turn of the head, a disdainful motion of the hand, the courtly cruel fashions of the past. Its stockings, like Prince Hamlet's, were ungartered, and there was that in the double disorder of its locks appropriate to both Pan and Lucifer. Mr. Hazard disliked the dark apparition in the arm-chair, and yet he could not deny his kinship to the thing. It was his mind; his spirit was another matter.

"Poor devil," said Mr. Hazard's mind, looking at his spirit. Mr. Hazard realized that the words were wrong; his mind knew better than that. "Poor angel" was the proper name for the fellow with the feathered shoulder-blades.

Mr. Hazard wondered where this pitiful spirit had found the plumes which drooped in languor at its sides; they might be goose-feathers from the pillow-case or ravellings from the void of heaven. It was impossible to be sure, because the creature was invested in a faint and tarnished splendour which nevertheless clouded its exact lineaments from view. It crouched on the narrow window-seat, its chin on its clasped hands, its silly pinions strewing the drab carpet with flakes of pearl. It seemed caught up into a trance of pain and amazement, and the loosened strings of its hair hung over its large eyes and blinded them.

"Hah! hah!" said Mr. Hazard's mind. "I congratulate you upon your collaborator. He did very well for you in the original Hebrew; doubtless it is his native tongue. But Mr. Hodge can crush him like an hour's ephemeron. I advise you to keep away from Lyonnesse while you have that fellow upon your hands. Mr. Hodge's boot-heel has no bowels of compassion."

"Will you be silent, intolerable demon?" asked Mr. Hazard without hope. He felt a lively sympathy for the creature on the window-seat, which shrank within its wings and trembled at the discourteous accents of the mind.

"Good-bye," said Mr. Hazard's mind, with a gesture of farewell. "Spend the morning upon the river; you are sadly in need of sleep. I will refrain from comment upon your success as a reformer or a father; I will not demand your reasons for coming to England, or an account of your plans and escapades. You know that you have no voice in politics, no rank in letters, no honourable station in the world. A pretty mess you and your winged ephemeron have made of the business of life; even your pursuit of ghosts has been a failure. Moths and may-flies. 'Dead flies cause the ointment of the apothecary to send forth a stinking savour. . . . A wise man's heart is at his right hand, but a fool's heart at his left.' A little folly, Mr. Hazard. Need I remind you of Allegra?"

"Please don't," said Mr. Hazard.

9

Crumbs for the Birds

Clara sat upon the terrace at Lyonnesse, bending her graceful head above twelve square inches of *petit point*. Her needle flashed in the sunlight and then stopped, quivering like a little arrow in the centre of a rose. The rose-coloured thread hung limp, not drawn into the mesh of the embroidery among the other stitches; Clara's hand remained poised in idleness. The star-sapphire which her father had given her shone like an evening planet against her hand.

She meditated; her eyes, which were bluer than the grey-blue jewel, searched the sky and returned to the *petit point*. She stabbed the rose to its heart and drew out the rose-coloured thread with deliberation.

"Here is a curious note from Mr. Hazard," she said to Mr. Hodge, who sat upon the balustrade. Mr. Hodge was pretending to correct Latin exercises, but under his heavy brows his eyes were never farther from Clara's face than the toe of her bronze slipper. "It was brought by hand from Gravelow; I suppose that means the absurd creature brought it himself, for he has nobody to run errands for him. It says . . . in substance . . . that he could not dine tonight. But it is so cryptic that I feel sure he is unwell."

"What is the matter with him?" asked Mr. Hodge, who knew without asking. "I thought he was never happy except at Lyonnesse. Is he beginning to tire of your hospitality?"

"From the tone of his note, I think he has rather languished for lack of it," said Clara, smiling. "His agitation is obvious. No, I won't show you the note, because you are certain to laugh at it. It is really a very odd note; it worries me."

"Then you had better let me see it, Lady Clara," said Mr. Hodge, looking chivalrous and solemn. "It is like the fellow's base ingratitude to worry you, who have been such a minister of grace to him. But it is of a piece with the rest of his impudence. You had far better let me see what he has written."

"Very well," said Clara, "but you are not to laugh at poor Mr. Hazard. He is not ungrateful, but I fear he is a little mad. There, you may see for yourself . . . only you mustn't look so scornful, Hodge, or I shall wish I had not let you see it."

Mr. Hodge took the note and read it slowly; in obedience to Clara's words he erased the sneer from his lips, but under his brows his eyes were hard and empty as a pair of grey shells. He had driven the contempt from his eyes at Clara's command; they were quite expressionless as he stared at Mr. Hazard's note.

"My dear friend," said the note, which was written in pencil, "I am sorry that I cannot dine with you tonight, but—

'Why, let the stricken deer go weep,
The hart ungallèd play;
For some must watch, while some must sleep:
Thus runs the world away.'

Believe me ever most sensible of your kindness."

"But he has not even taken the trouble to sign it!" cried Mr. Hodge in spite of himself. "And in pencil; it is inexcusable that he should write to you in pencil. It is written upon—what? A page from a tradesman's book?"

"A leaf from a note-book," said Clara with inaudible mockery. "He always writes on the leaves of note-books. And it doesn't matter about his name; I know his handwriting very well, you see."

"My God, how long must I bear this?" said Mr. Hodge under his breath; he did not dare to say the words aloud. He tried to keep his voice calm and monotonous as he spoke.

"But what a letter!" said Mr. Hodge. "What a disgusting letter for a grown man to write! If a schoolboy were guilty of such repulsive self-pity, I should think it my duty to cane him. Ah, Hamlet, forsooth! It is Hamlet, is it not, that the fool is quoting? And his friend, Lady Clara, his dear friend. Do you see that he addresses you as his friend?"

"That is no more than the truth, Hodge," said Clara with composure, "I am his friend; I have given him the right to address me as a friend. Pray keep your temper; it is a pity I allowed you to see the note. As to Hamlet—do you think he is serious? He is out of spirits, of course; I dare say, like Hamlet, he is a little mad, but I am sure he is laughing at himself in this letter. He is not quite such a fool as you would have him."

"I would not have him at any price, mad or sane, wise or foolish," said Mr. Hodge with controlled fury. "Forgive me, Lady Clara, but the man sickens me; I am not myself when I consider him. I had as lief see you with a toad in your hand as with that revolting letter."

"We have had enough hard words," said

Clara. "Let us try a few pearls and diamonds for a change. Now I am going to ask poor Mr. Hazard to dinner on Friday, and if you cannot promise to be kind and civil, then you must go and be rude elsewhere, for I will not tolerate it here. You might run up to London for the night to see the Water-colour Exhibition or to improve your mind with the Elgin marbles. Or do you prefer to be good and stay at home?"

"I shall be good, as you are pleased to call it," said Mr. Hodge, "but you are mistaken; I shall merely be hypocritical. If I followed the dictates of my conscience in this matter, I should . . ."

"Horsewhip Mr. Hazard, I suppose," said Clara laughing. "Ah, my dear Hodge, I know your prejudices too well; you are as narrow as my little finger-nail. Nevertheless you have a sterling character; perhaps your virtue has earned its prejudices. But you must be kind to Mr. Hazard."

"I was not going to say anything about horsewhips; I am not a bully," said Mr. Hodge with dignity. "You may depend upon it that my manners on Friday will be no worse than usual."

"Then I must be content with moderate

blessings," said Clara. "But listen; we will have turbot and a beautiful pair of ducks and the first of the raspberries; I may have a pineapple sent down from London. You shall choose the wines yourself, and drink them too, since the rest of us don't appreciate them. It will be a festival, a gala occasion; the girls shall put on their prettiest frocks, and I will wear white satin and sapphires. We will build a triumphal arch for Mr. Hazard with 'Friendship's Garland' woven thereon in roses; we will have Roman candles and rockets and set pieces; we will persuade Paganini to sing for his supper on the violin, and Taglioni shall dance for us under the moon. It will be a delightful party, and we shall all live happy ever after."

"There will be no moon on Friday night," said Mr. Hodge sombrely, "and please do not wear any more sapphires; you wear far too many for my peace of mind."

Clara blinked her blue eyes and pretended not to hear. She was relieved to know that Mr. Hodge's mood was softened by her chatter, and she began to feel much less worried about Mr. Hazard. After all, one could practise sorceries and glamours by means of a few words of nonsense and a promise of early raspberries. If Mr. Hazard were ill, a slice of duckling and a glass of white wine might be curative magic, and if he were melancholy-mad, it must inevitably medicine his spirits to see Rosa and Allegra in their prettiest frocks.

10

The Sage in Meditation

MR. HAZARD had set forth from Gravelow with every intention of dining at Lyonnesse; it was only when its actual tower shadowed the river at his right hand that his heart failed him. His fortitude went from him, and as the skiff left the sunlight and glided into the darkened stretch of water, he relapsed into doubt and sad self-questionings. A mist arose from the shaded water, and while his lungs received it, he inhaled misgiving and suspired his final breath of courage.

A small secretive beast slid from the bank into the river; its shape of vole or weasel was indistinguishable in the dusk. Whether the pursued or the pursuer, whether ravening or in flight, the thing was to be envied. The ripples of its course were soon dispersed; it was hidden in the glittering sunlit reach beyond. Mr. Hazard wished it well; for his own fate he could desire nothing better, unless indeed it were the lucky destiny of a stone or a tree rooted in green shallows. He rowed past the house, avoiding the high steps of the landing-place, and proceeding a little farther down the stream, he moored his boat in deep obscurity. He bent his eyes close above the pages of his note-book, and there in the mist and luminous eclipse of day he wrote a letter to Clara. He laughed as he wrote it, beholding a stricken water-rat fleeing like a deer to the remoter bank. "Thus runs the world away!" said Mr. Hazard to himself, with noiseless laughter. Thus runs the world, thus flows the river, running softly, thus run and flow the pulses of the blood, running in the wrist, in the hollow temple, and under the ribs at the left hand of a fool.

When Mr. Hazard had written the note, he scrambled up the bank and looked about him. He was no great distance from the house, and he considered going to the front door and leaving the note in his proper person. He had proceeded half-way along the flagged path when he caught sight of Clara and Mr. Hodge upon the terrace. Clara's hair was powdered to pale silver-gold by the twilight; she threw back her head, regarding her embroidery at arm's length, and her profile and the faint colour of her hair were Allegra's. Even in the dusk Mr. Hazard could see the contours of her face, clear, aerial, aquiline, lifted upon invisible wings of pride, shining with an inner flame of mockery.

Mr. Hazard's bones were turned to water, and this water did not run softly and smoothly like the river Thames; it was rather a subterranean stream of cataracts and rapids. He stood hidden in the shadows, quiet as one of the leaden figures bordering the path, quiet as the moss-grown satyr in the hedge. He was absorbed into the darkness about him; he was conscious only of the bitter smell of yew and the sweet smell of jasmine, and of the little note fluttering between his fingers like a living thing, while his fingers did not tremble, but remained stiff and cold as stone or lead. How should he move his hands to still the fluttering of the note, or his feet to proceed along the path, when his bones were turned to water within the body of a leaden satyr?

Mr. Hazard was spared the trouble of delivering his note; a man emerged from the dusk carrying a flat basket of roses on his arm. He was evidently a gardener; he stared at Mr. Hazard for a moment, and then civilly demanded his business. Mr. Hazard gave him the letter with instructions to convey it to the house at once; he gave the gardener a piece of silver, and the man touched his cap and left him. The incident proved his own humanity to Mr. Hazard; he perceived that he was alive, that he was after all a person capable of tipping servants and imposing his will on fellow mortals. He turned and walked with swift and resilient steps along the way he had come. He was no longer afraid of meeting Allegra; he knew that he would not meet her upon this retired path. When a white owl swooped from the shadows like a waning moon, Mr. Hazard was not halted in his light and even stride. Nevertheless he had been both lonely and afraid during that long moment while he stood like a leaden statue in the dusk, moveless except for the quick processes of his mind and the fluttering of the note between his fingers. He had felt remote from the comfortable bonds of flesh and blood, coldly and strangely severed from his kinship with mankind. The gardener had given him back the common stamp of humanity; he was glad of the assurance. Mr. Hazard thought he had purchased it cheaply with a single piece of silver, and he was sorry he had not given the man five shillings instead of half a crown.

He rowed slowly up the river to Gravelow; he rowed against the current and against the inner wishes of his heart, which were turned backward to Lyonnesse. Yet he knew that he could never have faced Clara and her children without some stupid blunder upon the part of his soul; he would have been stiff and cold as a statue, or, worse, he would have been a silly wild beast, struck in the side by a shaft of ridicule and dislike, ashamed of its wound, frantic for solitude. No, it was far wiser to go home; to go home to Gravelow.

"Hah," said Mr. Hazard, aware of his own weakness. " 'Why, let the stricken deer go weep' ... by all means, and in decent seclusion." He thought of Mr. Hodge's sleek dark head, bent over Latin exercises, while Clara regarded her bright embroidery at arm's length. "'The hart ungallèd play . . .'" He rowed faster, rowing until he was out of breath and almost out of the memory of Lyonnesse and the power of its spell. He rowed until he was blind and breathless, rowing away from Lyonnesse.

The next morning the spell had reassumed its power. About eleven o'clock Susan brought him a note, waiting by the door while he read it. "There's an answer," said Susan. "The man says there's an answer, sir, and you're please to send it back by him."

"Friday," said Mr. Hazard to himself, reading the note, "Day after tomorrow. I am to come without fail. Am I sure I am quite well? Isn't the weather delicious? The little girls have learned Hummel's duet sonata in E flat. Till Friday, she is mine most truly, Clara Hunting. Postscript. I am not to work too hard at what's-his-name."

"You needn't wait, Susan," said Mr. Hazard, "I'll bring the answer down myself when I've written it. Tell the man I shan't be five seconds."

It took him less than five seconds to make up his mind. Suddenly he knew the measure of his ingratitude and vanity. He laughed with joy to know himself mistaken, selfish, ill-conditioned; the knowledge relieved despair like a draught of sacrament. Knowing Clara right and himself wilfully wrong, the world swung round upon a noble axis, and the sun was once more within its proper quarter of the sky. The morning rose, expanding like a tree, towards the heights of noon; all sounds and odours grew clear and delicate, and the simple forms of earth were moulded with nicety and justice. The smallest leaf that hung against his window was scalloped and veined according to divine sanction.

Mr. Hazard wrote his answer to Clara in seven words, and ran downstairs to give it to the servant. Remembering that he had not rewarded the gardener as the man deserved, he put all his silver coins into this other servant's hands. It was extravagant, but not so extravagant as it might have been had Mr. Hazard ever carried many coins in his pocket, either of silver or gold.

11

A Fine Pair of Sapphires

"Of course we will come, if Mama will let us," said Rosa. "Afternoon tea in Gravelow; it sounds lovely. Perhaps we might have the horses that afternoon, and come very grandly in the carriage; then we could wear our best clothes and be elegant young ladies, while the boys and Mr. Hodge go by way of the river. But wait; we must ask Mama."

"I had meant," said Mr. Hazard rather diffidently, "to ask your mother to do me the honour of coming with you next Wednesday. Perhaps it is too much to hope for, but it would be so very much happier a solution of the chaperon problem than a governess can ever be, and then . . . to have her with us . . . but I suppose it is impossible. In fact, I suppose the whole scheme is impossible; it is too charming to come true."

"Well," said Rosa, "we must ask her; she cannot be angry with you for asking. I am afraid she will say no, but then you won't be worse off than you are now, and she might just conceivably say yes, mightn't she?"

"Do you think she might?" asked Mr. Hazard; he looked at Clara, and her smile, and the meek fashion of her parted hair, and the sapphire dangling against her cheek, and the softer, more merciful jewels of her eyes, informed him of her kindness. He rose and crossed the terrace to her chair, and drew another chair close to it, and, choosing his words very carefully, he asked her to drink tea with him next Wednesday afternoon.

Mr. Hodge, who sat upon the balustrade between Tristram and Allegra, could not hear Mr. Hazard's carefully chosen words, but he could hear the absurd vibration of Mr. Hazard's nerves made audible in his voice. Mr. Hazard was nervous; he had set his heart upon persuading Clara to say yes instead of no, and now his heart was in his mouth and evident in the uneven sound of his voice. Mr. Hodge wondered what the fool was saying with such unnecessary fervour; it might have been a declaration of love or an appeal against a capital sentence.

It was both; Mr. Hazard felt his destiny dependent upon Clara's nod, which would let her sapphire ear-rings fall forward in line with her eyelashes, or the shake of her head, which would fling them sparkling from side to side. He watched her face, his thin hands gripping the carven bosses of the chair.

"You see," explained Mr. Hazard, "it shouldn't be such an unfair division of pleasures. You have given, and given again and again, and I have taken your charity and brought nothing in return."

"Hospitality," said Clara, "and of the simplest sort. Please don't call it charity, Mr. Hazard; you make me feel as if I had been giving you soup and flannels."

She laughed, and Mr. Hazard laughed with her, but Mr. Hodge could have sworn that there was no conviction in the fellow's lunatic mirth.

"You have," said Mr. Hazard, "food and raiment, and these for a starving man. It is charity, and sheer munificence; I have nothing to give you in exchange. But if you would allow me to have a tea-party for the children; a tea-party seems the only possible thing for summer. If it were winter, I suppose there would still be pantomimes. But by next winter I shall be in Spain."

It was the forlorn echoes in the last sentence which decided Clara, and the inevitable ring of parting in the last word. Spain was distant enough, in reality, and Mr. Hazard's voice made it sound more distant than the moon. Clara, who had once glanced into *The Conquest of Granada*, had a picture of Mr. Hazard sitting lonely as Boabdil in a small Moorish palace, while happier people went to pantomimes. Also, she remembered that by September Mr. Hazard would be on his way to Spain; she would be sorry to see the poor creature go, and yet she knew that his going would lift a little burden from her mind and cut the trivial knot of perplexities tangled about his presence.

"Very well," she said sweetly; her ear-rings swung forward as she bowed her head in consent. Her smile was teasing and lenient; her sidelong glance at Mr. Hazard observed that his fingers had relaxed upon the arms of his chair. His sigh of relief touched her lightly with amusement and pity. He looked at Allegra, and Clara looked away.

When Mr. Hazard had gone home that

evening, Mr. Hodge was afraid to ask Clara any questions. He wondered very much what cause Mr. Hazard had been pleading as he leaned towards Clara, his knuckles white against the arms of his chair, his voice tense and uneven. Mr. Hodge found it difficult to believe the ridiculous truth when he heard it, and yet the truth displeased him.

"Is that the vastly important project he was discussing?" asked Mr. Hodge. "I thought it was a life-and-death matter, that he had got his precious neck in jeopardy or was planning an elopement to the Cyclades. A tea-party! How infantile! At the same time, Lady Clara, I doubt your wisdom in having yielded to his wishes. You are too tender-hearted; he imposes upon you at every turn."

Clara could not help laughing, though Mr. Hodge's vehemence annoyed her. "Thank you," she said, "I do not like insults to my common sense, my dear Hodge, even as the price of compliments to my kind heart. If Mr. Hazard is capable of imposing upon me, I must be amazingly simple-minded. I assure you that if the poor darling had a little pane of glass set in that speculative brow of his, his thoughts could be no plainer to me than they are."

"I am glad to hear it," said Mr. Hodge, "I am glad to know that you cannot by any chance be deceived in his character."

"But he is such an innocent creature, Hodge!" said Clara. "He is clever enough at writing verse, I suppose, but he knows nothing of the world. It is stupid of you to talk as if he were a sort of Lovelace. Am I a silly Clarissa, a simpleton of fifteen? I tell you I can wind him round my little finger like this poor bit of black silk."

"But he is wound about Allegra's little finger," said Mr. Hodge solemnly. "It is Allegra whom he loves, Lady Clara; that has been ludicrously clear from the beginning."

Clara looked at Mr. Hodge, and in the thin summer darkness her amethystine eyes were inscrutable. Slowly she unwound the strand of black silk from about her little finger and allowed it to drift to the grass at her feet. She lifted her hand, and the sapphire rings upon her fingers caught the starlight and held it.

"Ah, Hodge, why need you have said that?"

she asked softly. "I am sorry you said it in so
many words. It is cruel to define these things too
plainly; we must pretend they aren't true, if they
are sad enough, and there is no help for them.
I have not said it so plainly even to myself, and
I am sure Mr. Hazard has never dreamed of saying it."

"Then so much the worse for Mr. Hazard,"
said Mr. Hodge. "He has no moral honesty; he
refuses to face the bare facts of existence. His passion is laughable, but it is none the less dangerous
for being undignified."

"It is not laughable," said Clara gravely. "It
is a pitiable passion, if passion it is. We may smile
at these things while they remain unsaid, but you
have broken our poor conspiracy of silence. Yes,
yes, of course he is in love with Allegra; I, too,
have known it from the beginning, but it is so
deplorable that I have tried to pretend it isn't true.
I have played a harmless comedy to save his
pride."

"Surely it would have been kinder . . ." began Mr. Hodge, but Clara interrupted him impatiently. She was angry with him for making

her cry; she dabbed at her eyes with a fine lace handkerchief, reflecting that her handkerchiefs were not accustomed to tears. Tears were a rare indulgence with Clara; she thought them more expensive than the amber essence with which her handkerchief was scented.

"It would not have been kinder," she said with spirit. "It would have been the most malicious cruelty I could have contrived to hurt him. He does not like to be pitied, you know; nobody likes to be pitied. Do not insist upon turning my comedy into a tragedy by making me pity Mr. Hazard."

"As you please," said Mr. Hodge. "Your policy of blissful ignorance has much to recommend it to the moral coward. But for myself I prefer to face the issue at all costs. You pay a doubtful compliment to your Mr. Hazard in obscuring the truth."

"But I thought he was Allegra's Mr. Hazard," said Clara. "Thank you for making me laugh again, Hodge; tears have always bored me to distraction. It is an heroic portrait you draw of yourself; Haydon would be glad of it for his next historical piece. Let us stop quarrelling and be friends; there are no issues to be faced between friends. Only, you must not dot your i's and cross your t's in this tiresome manner, for it turns all life into a moral lesson."

"Good-night, Hodge," said Clara with recovered gaiety. "You must come to poor Mr. Hazard's tea-party with me next Wednesday. But, remember, never cross your t's until you come to them."

"How frivolous she is!" thought Mr. Hodge, staring at the sapphire heavens, whose infinite mocking brilliance was after all no more inscrutable than Clara's dark blue eyes.

12

Less Than Archangel Ruined

In Gravelow at this time there lived a woman who kept a small bakery in West Street. This woman was half Saxon peasant and half gipsy; she was neither young nor old, neither handsome nor notably plain. She was the sort of woman who keeps her shop-window in good order, but may possibly drink a little gin in secret.

Mr. Hazard was easily touched to pity or disgust; he was the sort of man who saves a commonplace woman from a burning house at the casual cost of his own life, but is spiritually exhausted by a quarter of an hour's conversation with her. Had he met her in a ditch, he would have shared his last crust with her, but he might have refused to employ her as kitchen-maid because she had ugly hands.

He was a connoisseur of obsidian and sardonyx; at a glance he could tell the Etruscan from the Island gems, and smile at one of Pichler's eighteenth-century Psyches. But he could not tell a stale rock-cake from a fresh one, or yesterday's buns from today's. The woman was an excellent pastry-cook, but she had rarely been able to resist the temptation to turn a dishonest halfpenny. She was therefore precisely the woman to sell yesterday's cream buns, and Mr. Hazard was precisely the man to buy them.

"A dozen buns, if you please," said Mr. Hazard, not asking for any particular kind of bun, or even inquiring the price. He looked very tall, and although his eyes were preternaturally bright, they gazed through the ceiling of the shop and ignored the cakes upon the counter.

The woman felt well-disposed towards Mr. Hazard; nevertheless she sold him a dozen of her most undesirable buns, wrapping them in a trim brown-paper parcel. "Thank you, sir," she said civilly, as she put his money into the till.

Mr. Hazard walked home to his lodgings; it was three o'clock of as exquisite an afternoon as even his fastidious taste could have chosen. If some power had permitted him selection among all the days of that July, if he had been allowed to turn them over beneath his hand like a heap of roses varying from warm to white, his preference must have fallen upon this afternoon. With honey at its core, and powdered grains of gold like fine Arabian spices dusting its inner leaves, the flower of this afternoon was cool and cloud-coloured; its blowing fringes were silver in the wind. It would not rain, and the wind blowing from the west could be trusted to blow the petals of light towards Gravelow. Mr. Hazard was content with his afternoon.

The true flowers in the green glass vases

perished in the confined space of his sitting-room; as soon as he entered the room, he perceived that the flowers were dying. He had cut them himself in the small garden, and putting them into the watery glass, he had forgotten to pour actual water upon their stems. Now they were drooping and dying in the tall green vases. He rang for Susan, who brought a jug of water to refresh them; her face was grave and doubtful as she looked at the flowers.

Mr. Hazard was not used to gathering flowers; in other years ladies had gathered flowers for him, but he preferred to leave a rose upon its stalk. He hoped that the cold water would revive the stems of these flowers.

"I tidied up a bit, as you told me to, sir," said Susan. "I'm afraid some of your books and papers may be hard to find in those pigeon-holes, but they're all safe, and the place looks beautiful. Did you remember the seed-cake, sir?"

"No," said Mr. Hazard, "I forgot it. Did you tell me to buy a seed-cake, Susan?"

"Yes, sir," said Susan, "but it doesn't matter. Everything will be very nice; we've got some lovely raspberries for you. Here's a letter, sir, come by the last post."

Mr. Hazard took the letter, believing that it came from Clara. The habitual pallor of his complexion was increased until he was as white as the thin sheaves of paper thrust into the pigeon-holes of the desk. He sat down on the edge of the desk and forced himself to look at the letter. The London postmark saved him from the tiresome necessity of fainting.

Susan was appalled. She had seen Mr. Hazard painfully affected by trifles, but she had never seen him overthrown as now. "Are you quite well, sir?" asked Susan, being very sure that he was ill.

"Quite," said Mr. Hazard rather crossly. "Please don't bother me, Susan; go downstairs and wait until I ring for you."

The letter was from Annamaria. The Hartleighs had not gone to Hythe after all; they were still in Marylebone. Also, they were in trouble. Annamaria hated to worry her dear Hazard while he was engaged upon his lyric drama, but as a matter of fact poor Hartleigh had the influenza. The boys were with a friend in Cornwall; the younger children had been sent to the Isle of Wight. These summer influenzas were particularly distressing. Hartleigh was miserable, and they were in serious financial difficulties.

At this moment Mr. Hazard heard the carriage coming along West Street; it drew up before his door with a clatter of hoofs and a smart jingle of harness. The coachman cracked his whip for no reason, and Tristram's laughter sounded, cold and bright as sleigh-bells in the summer air. Mr. Hazard crammed the letter into his pocket and rang furiously for Susan. He stood waiting, his face turned towards the door; his veins were filled with a fever of impatience, and all the while the letter uncurled itself in his pocket with a crackling noise like fire.

Mr. Hodge came into the room, followed by Tristram and Hilary; the passage was empty behind them and there were no more footsteps on the stairs.

"Where . . . ?" said Mr. Hazard, and felt the question stick in his throat like a sharp fishbone. All words were knives and splinters in his throat, and he was silent.

"Lady Clara decided not to come this afternoon," said Mr. Hodge; his manner was courteous and even gentle. "She feared that it might rain. Also her brother is arriving from Camphile Eden tonight, and she has various arrangements to make for his comfort. But she has sent us in her stead; we are the bearers of many apologies and regrets."

"The girls sent you their special love, Mr. Hazard," said Hilary. "They think it's very bad luck that they're not allowed to come with us."

"I've a note for you from my mother," said Tristram; the exquisite arrogance of his bearing was tempered by a cool and friendly smile. He turned out his pockets one by one, and found several notes, but not the note for Mr. Hazard.

"I'm frightfully sorry," said Tristram, "I must have lost it, or else she forgot to give it to me. I'm frightfully sorry, Mr. Hazard. Perhaps she gave it to you, Hodge."

"Never mind," said Mr. Hazard, who felt their blue eyes like so many knives at his throat. He knew that they had told him all that the note could say, and yet he wished that Tristram had not lost that scrap of Clara's handwriting.

Susan came in with the tea; she had cut the bread and butter delicately thin and piled the raspberries into a pyramid of damask. The cream buns were stale, but Susan hoped that Mr. Hazard would not eat any cream buns.

Mr. Hazard ate nothing at all. He knew that Susan had spread a large tea upon his writing-table; he wished that she had not filled the quiet of his room with tea-kettles and plates and spoons. He was sincerely grateful to Mr. Hodge for pouring out the tea.

13

A Moonstone Intaglio

THE boys made an excellent tea; the cream buns disappointed them, but the perfection of the raspberries more than atoned for this. Mr. Hodge ate a slice of bread and butter, and looked at Mr. Hazard. Mr. Hazard seemed quite unaware of his duty as a host.

"You had better have a cup of tea," said Mr. Hodge in a kindly voice, his hand upon the teapot. Mr. Hodge did not like pouring out tea, but he realized that Mr. Hazard was, for the moment, incapable of the effort. There was no use in their all going hungry because Mr. Hazard had been born a pitiful fool.

"No, thank you," said Mr. Hazard, who was not hungry. He watched the faces of the boys, their slight aquiline features, the freckles gold against the bright colour on their cheek-bones. He listened to their animated tones and to the running chorus of Tristram's laughter. He was glad that they were making such an excellent tea, but he longed for Clara's note that Tristram had forgotten.

Mr. Hodge was speaking to him in a low portentous voice, which was tuned to darker secrets than the children's voices. Mr. Hazard turned to him, hearing the end of the world in the heavy reverberations of that voice.

"She thought it wiser not to come, and more considerate of your feelings," said Mr. Hodge. "I assured her that you would understand; you would not wish to cause a moment's disquietude to Allegra's mother. You do understand, don't you?"

"Of course," said Mr. Hazard. It was true;

Mr. Hazard understood, and the thing that Mr. Hazard understood grew clearer than the air and more exactly carven than the moon's shell within the glass of an astronomer.

It was not the end of the world; it was the strange countenance of the moon, brought close, and staring with calm-lidded eyes at Mr. Hazard. Mr. Hazard's own eyes were supernaturally turned into a pair of star-gazing crystals, and his perceptions were increased to angelic power. He knew rather more than he wanted to know, but the thing that he knew was familiar, now that he saw it clearly in the glass.

He understood that Mr. Hodge believed him to be in love with Allegra. This was inevitable and to be forgiven; he had believed it himself until the last instant, although he had never confessed it to his mind. He had loved Allegra in the first moment of beholding her; nay, he had adored her with the burning remnant of his flesh and the insensate passions of his spirit. He had starved and thirsted for lack of her; he had accepted dry crumbs and dew-drop morsels in place of food, and been satisfied with deprivation. Moved by this true radical force of love, he had harnessed mountains and broken them to his rein and cut a path from the cold extreme of heaven. He had made his love an Archimedean lever whereby the world was tilted one degree nearer to the universal good. These things he had accomplished, knowing that she would not care a silver pin for such wonders, and she had not cared.

She had not cared, and his accomplishment had wearied him, and his love for Allegra had fallen into a decline, and died of languor and exhaustion. Dry crumbs and dew-drops are thin fare to support the vitality of the heart, and while his starved and baffled love lay dying, Clara had come to Mr. Hazard and stood at his left hand, a little apart, not smiling, not pitying him or seeming to divine his pain. He had loved her for this and he loved her still; it was possible that he would always love her. He was sure that she was aware of this, and that, upon the whole, she considered it a compliment.

What else she knew could only be conjectured; certainly he would never ask her, but if he were to ask her a hundred times, he would get no more than the least fraction of a smile for answer. Perhaps her graceful and neglectful air, the bright eyes turned the other way, the light mind absent upon more amusing errands, had been delicate acts of mercy; perhaps they had been simple laziness. She had watched the entire course of his ridiculous and tragic love without a sign; she had blinked her dark blue eyes and played tricks with the musical stops of her voice, and by means of these innocent diversions she had won him from despair. She had seen him look to her from Allegra, and still she had given no sign, and by means of pretence she had kept his pride inviolate and saved his face. He hated his face, and yet while its precarious mask was fitted round his mind, it assured him a little privacy. He loved Clara for saving his face, even if she had done it to save trouble for herself.

Mr. Hazard remembered Clara, and a pang of intense desire cut his heart in two. He longed for the woman in ten thousand idle ways which, being added together and summed up, became a crying hunger, an instinctive need, an immediate infantile wailing within the spirit. What difference, earthly or divine, did it make to Mr. Hazard whether Clara were invested in supernal wisdom or in the careless and enchanting attributes of flesh and blood? She had been his friend and saviour, and now he loved the narrow ground she walked upon, although she might be a mere piece of that fair ground, a lady of clay. Perhaps she was a goddess and had contrived it all from above, but he suspected her strongly of being a woman, and he loved her better for the fault. He longed for the bit of paper whereon her hand had inscribed a set of gentle and untrue excuses for failing him today.

Mr. Hazard saw that Mr. Hodge and the boys were going; he rose and said good-bye to them with fluency and ease. The engaging manners of his youth returned for a moment, like a ghostly reflection, to flicker in his lips and eyes. For this brief moment he was as polite as Hilary, as witty as Tristram, and several inches taller than Mr. Hodge.

He stood with his hands in his trousers' pockets, regarding the others with a faintly meta-physical smile. His fingers touched Annamaria's letter, and he drew it forth. He had forgotten it, and yet it was precisely what he had been needing for the past three minutes.

"I have had a letter from London," he said to Mr. Hodge, "which calls me away at once upon important business. The business will be long and complicated, and although it may only take me to Marylebone, it may quite conceivably take me to Abyssinia. As I leave Gravelow tomorrow, I am afraid I shall not see Lady Clara again before next summer."

The breath was knocked from Mr. Hodge's magnificent chest by these amazing words; he was incredulous of his facile triumph. The boys' young voices were lifted in a babble of surprise, but Mr. Hodge was unable to speak. He was a sceptic, and yet he thanked the author of this blessing in a mood of religious awe. Doubtless, thought Mr. Hodge, its true author was the beautiful Clara Hunting, that gold and ivory image of his idolatry. Yet he spared an approving glance for Tristram, for Tristram had lost his mother's note to Mr. Hazard. It is impossible for a poor mortal to foretell with any degree of certainty the oracular message that a gold and ivory image may compress into a small three-cornered note.

"If you are leaving tomorrow, you will want to pack," said Mr. Hodge rather unsteadily. He looked at the books, at the accumulated rows of Greek poets and Hebrew prophets and kings. He looked at Mr. Hazard; an actual sensation of pity caught him unprepared. Mr. Hazard was teetering back and forth on his heels and toes and smiling a secret philosophical smile, but to Mr. Hodge's eyes he looked more than ever a contemptible anatomy. He was as thin as a storm-bitten scarecrow and as pale as a rain-washed rag.

"Don't you want me to help you pack those books?" asked Mr. Hodge, stirred by an humane impulse. "There are a tremendous lot of them, you know; you'll find it rather a job to finish by yourself."

Mr. Hazard looked at Mr. Hodge; he saw plainly that Mr. Hodge was moved by a laudable impulse, but he also saw that such an impulse would never have moved Mr. Hodge had Mr. Hazard not been going to London tomorrow.

Mr. Hazard had scared away a multitude of crows by his blacker pride; he opened his smiling lips to emit a politely scornful negative, and then thought better of it. After all, he felt wretchedly tired and ill; there were far too many dying flowers in the room, and the windows had never been wide enough. Why should he hesitate to employ Mr. Hodge's excess and prodigality of muscle to perform those gross gymnastics which must wear the body to its death and leave the soul unstrengthened? For years he had worn away the precious metal of his body by such trumpery pains.

"It would be pure good nature upon your part to help me," said Mr. Hazard with his smallest and most subliminal smile. He raised his fine ironic eyebrows, and began to sort his books into neat and rational piles. He was very careful to lay his own fragile sallow hands upon none save the slenderer volumes; he left all the heavier and duller books to Mr. Hodge. He put the *Symposium* and *Paradise Lost* into his two coat-pockets, and dropped Miss Barrett's *Prometheus Bound* into the waste-paper-basket. His white vellum set of the

Greek dramatists went next to Shelley and Coleridge in the pigskin box.

So soon as the exertion of packing had wearied Mr. Hazard, which happened within five minutes of his first effort, he sank into the most comfortable arm-chair that the room afforded and observed Mr. Hodge with sympathetic interest. Mr. Hodge was very hot; his sleek dark hair had fallen into his eyes, and his broadcloth coat would have fared better upon the back of a chair than stretched across Mr. Hodge's splendid shoulders. Mr. Hazard examined the cluster of seals upon his watch-chain, and, choosing the most curious, detached it from the rest.

"Tristram," he said in his light dry voice, "may I impose upon your memory in so far as to ask you to give this little intaglio to your mother? It is a pretty antique; a Greek scarabæoid of the happiest period. Beg her to accept it as a token of my gratitude and an earnest of my friendship, and bid her good-bye until next summer, or perhaps until a later day."

Tristram looked critically at the seal which Mr. Hazard had given him; it appeared to be a blond and frosted moonstone, bearing upon its surface the figures of a lion and a stag. The lion's teeth were sunk in the stag's flying shoulder; the gem itself was clipped by a worn silver band.

"I will show it to my mother," said Tristram rather haughtily, "but I don't believe she will wish to take it, Mr. Hazard. It is too valuable to be given away."

"Do you think so, Tristram?" asked Mr. Hazard with his imperceptible smile.

He sat in the small room, among the dying constellations of the flowers, among the teacups glimmering like sea-shells on the table, with the three restless presences fixed opposite him in the disorder of the place. Hilary whistled the march from *Faniska* and drummed with his fingers upon the straitened window frames; Tristram frowned over the intaglio seal; Mr. Hodge sweated at his labours. Mr. Hazard leaned his head against the comfortable cushions of his chair; the intellectual colour of his eyes was full of laughter.

He knew that tomorrow, in the London coach, he would feel faint and suffocated among its odours of mortality, and crossed in love and fortune, but for the moment he was happy. There were five points to a star; these three uneasy presences were in the room, and himself, making four, and a fifth which set a crown upon the whole and was superior to the others and remained a part of heaven.